MW01658242

"This has been hard on you, I know," Track told her

The senator's daughter shrugged as Track cut away the remnants of the cord that had bound her hands to the pommel of the saddle.

She stood behind him as he worked, and he smiled when he heard her say, "It's too bad you and I were never able to get it on, Mr.—Dan."

Track shook his head. "To tell you the truth, honey, either you're a little too young for me, or I'm a little too old for you. But don't think I'm not flattered."

He had the last rope cut and turned to face her—just in time to see the rock as it hammered toward his head.

Now available in the exciting new series from Gold Eagle Books

TRACK

by Jerry Ahern

#1 The Ninety-Nine
#2 Atrocity
#3 The Armageddon Conspiracy
#4 The Hard Way
#5 Origin of a Vendetta
#6 Certain Blood
#7 Master of D.E.A.T.H.
#8 Revenge of the Master
#9 The D.E.A.T.H. Hunters
#10 Cocaine Run

TRACK
Cocaine Run

JERRY AHERN

A GOLD EAGLE BOOK FROM
WORLDWIDE

TORONTO • NEW YORK • LONDON • PARIS
AMSTERDAM • STOCKHOLM • HAMBURG
ATHENS • MILAN • TOKYO • SYDNEY

For all the people who have written, called, stopped by at autographings to say that they like Dan Track—this one's for you, with all the best.

First edition December 1985

ISBN 0-373-62010-1

Printed in Canada.

1

The sun was incredibly hot; he would have removed his white rumpled suit jacket if it hadn't been for the shoulder holster. But as Fritz Cheatum stepped under the archway, he was suddenly cool. The sun gone, a damp-smelling draft filtered toward him through the hundred yards or so of wide, arch-covered breezeway that led between the gray and brown disintergrating stuccoed buildings. As he walked, he reached into his hip pocket for his handkerchief; like everything in contact with his body—even his gun, he imagined—the handkerchief was wet and clammy. He squeezed it in his fist and then smoothed it out as he ambled on, using the cloth to mop his brow.

Cheatum hated the tropics. Even as a child he had hated summer except for the fact that you were released from school then. Cold breezes—he liked the best. He walked on, stuffing his handkerchief into his right hip pocket.

And then Fritz Cheatum stopped walking. He stared and cursed his stupidity. His right hand, still in his hip pocket, would reach the Beretta 84 in time. "Hey, man, look...ah..."

"Kiss your ass goodbye, hombre." The burly bearded man shoved the pistol forward. Mechanically, as Fritz Cheatum tried for the .380 under his armpit anyway, he recognized the gun that was trained on him. It was a Colt Woodsman Sport .22, and the thing that looked like a black, petrified hotdog attached to the muzzle was a silencer. At the trigger end was Enrique—the single name by which the assassin was known.

The sound wasn't the ones silencers made in the movies at all, Cheatum thought, as he fell closing his eyes.

ENRIQUE PUMPED THE TRIGGER of the Woodsman twice more, watching as the DEA man's body twitched with the bullets' impact. *"Mierda,"* he flung out. He turned and walked along the breezeway. The Woodsman was a great little pistol; with the silencer on, it was as silent as you could get without special ammunition and a slide lock. But it was a damned nuisance to clean. He'd give it to the kid to clean, he decided. The kid enjoyed doing it.

He left the breezeway, the Woodsman and silencer under his shirt, the gun already coated with sweat. A woman—she looked part Negro—walked past the arched breezeway. Her hair was covered with a rag, faded blue like the dress that hung on her skinny body in wrinkled folds. He sneered at the woman and walked on. No one would stop him. No one would inform on him. They all knew what had happened to the others.

As he made his way toward the white 1978 Ford LTD parked at the end of the street, he thought about the DEA man. Enrique smiled. He remembered his first gun, stolen from a cop he'd killed with a pop bottle in an alley when he'd just turned thirteen. Now some kid would come along—but only a kid with guts—and turn out Cheatum's pockets for money. Then he'd find whatever gun Cheatum had been reaching for.

It gave Enrique a good feeling. He'd stolen his first gun after making the kill himself. It would be easier for this kid. The hard part of it was already done for him.

As he stopped at the car door Enrique shook his head. Kids these days had so much done for them. How could anyone blame the younger generation for turning out the way they did?

He opened the car door and turned the key in the ignition. He never locked his car and he always left the keys in the ignition switch. It was a statement, of sorts. As he often said, "Take a real gold-plated asshole to boost my car." Enrique moved the selector into drive, glanced at the mirror and turned into the street. He made a U-turn past the sign that said not to and accelerated.

He took the first right, accelerating again and shooting a wave to the police jeep and Rudolpho Ruiz behind the wheel. Rudolpho waved back.

Enrique took the left two blocks down onto the highway, hammering his foot down on the gas pedal—it had taken a little while longer than he'd thought to nail Cheatum and he was running late.

With the LTD's front and rear windows open on both sides, the slipstream howled at his ears, tore at his hair, billowed his half-open shirt and dried some of the sweat in the matted hair on his chest. It felt good.

After he'd bought the LTD, he'd had the speedometer pulled and a real one installed. The original speedometer only read up to eighty-five miles per hour, but the first time he'd floored the Ford he knew it could do better than that. He checked the speedometer now with more than a little pride. The 302 V-8 had been turned and revved to get everything out of the engine that was possible. The pollution garbage had been removed. The speedometer read accurately just under 105.

He took the wheel in his left hand and hit the radio knob. "Fuckin' mariachi crap," he snarled. He missed New York where he'd grown up. You could get decent rock music up there.

Enrique slowed, letting the rear end fishtail a little as he turned off the paved road onto the dirt driveway and started to accelerate. The white house loomed above and ahead of him. He looked at his new gold Rolex President. He'd broken the last one on some guy's face in a bar two weeks ago. This one was running okay. He was only ten minutes late.

The gravel driveway began to get steeper and he slowed the LTD a little, taking the curve right and smelling dust. The rear end shimmied a little. He made a mental note to have it checked. Meanwhile he slowed still more because Vasquez always complained about ruts in the driveway.

He took the turn into the horseshoe and stomped the brake pedal, throwing the transmission into park. The full-size American car was still rocking as he stepped out. He slammed the door behind him and walked around the rear of the vehicle and toward the stone steps at the front of the house. He took the steps three at a time. The kid was sitting cross-legged beside the front door.

"Here kid—shoot some rats, huh?" and he drew the Woodsman and whacked the butt of it into the kid's outstretched left hand.

"*Muchas gracias,* Enrique."

"Yeah—*nada*—clean it up, huh," and he tousled the boy's black hair. The kid was skinny, and the once-white T-shirt and the faded cut-off shorts hung on his bony frame.

Enrique turned the knob on the front door and left the kid behind as he slammed it after him. He patted his right side under his shirt—the little S&W .66 was where it always was.

He crossed the entrance hall and took the steps leading to the second floor two at a time, hearing the woman from downstairs calling after him, "You're fifteen minutes late, slob!"

Enrique shouted over his shoulder, without looking at her, "Fuck you, Madelaine." He reached the landing and slowed his pace. He swept back his mane of black hair, then smoothed down his beard. He walked briskly to the end of the hall on the left and stopped at the door there. Enrique decided to do up one more shirt button for appearance sake.

Then with the knuckles of his massive left hand he rapped on the door.

"Enrique?"

Enrique opened the door and stepped into the room. "Yeah, Mr. Vasquez. Look, ah—sorry about bein' late—*lo siento*, huh?"

As he watched Vasquez's face his eyes strayed to his gray-blue hair, the color chosen by old ladies. He wondered if Vasquez's hair was dyed.

"Come here and sit," Vasquez snapped.

Enrique started across the faded carpet, toward the paper-littered desk. Vasquez looked hispanic, the name was hispanic but Enrique had never heard Vasquez speak anything but English. New York English all the way. Enrique guessed that was why he put up with Vasquez—Vasquez reminded him of New York. Enrique stood in front of the desk for a moment then plopped into the chair. "So I croaked the DEA guy good. He even recognized me!"

"Wonderful. Maybe DEA's startin' a goddamned fan club for ya—ya took care of so many of their guys already. Anyways, I got a job for ya."

Enrique breathed out. "Look, Mr. Vasquez, I figured to take a few days, ya know, maybe take the kid fishin', huh?"

"That goddamn kid keeps hanging out outside this house, I swear, man you gonna go fishin' for him instead of with him."

"Hey, look—he's a good kid, Mr. Vasquez."

"Makes the house look worse than it is. Kick his ass outa here or I will."

Enrique figured it was best to change the subject. "What's the job, Mr. Vasquez?"

Vasquez looked up from his paperwork, the whites around his brown eyes yellowish and old looking. "What the fuck ya think it is?"

"Who, Mr. Vasquez?"

Vasquez threw down his Bic pen and picked up a half-crushed package of Winstons and fired one with a wind lighter. "Okay. I want ya to take care of Bastogne."

"Bastogne?"

"Bastogne—and quick."

"Jeez, Mr. Vasquez, you want the fuckin' commies down our necks?"

Vasquez exhaled a thin stream of smoke through his nostrils. "I cleared it with Halston and he cleared it with General Fuentes. Bastogne's gotta go. You're doin' it. Take somebody with ya, ya need help, huh? Bastongne's visiting his mother over at her farm in the next province. Wipe her out, too. Right?"

"I don't like killin' somebody's mother, Mr. Vasquez. Ain't right, ya know?"

"Kill him, kill her. Then torch the farmhouse. Fuentes'll take care of any problems. Then get yourself across the border into Mexico and take some time off, huh?" Vasquez stubbed the cigarette, then smiled. "Go take the kid with ya, if ya want, huh? I'm good-hearted. Just don't bring the little bastard back 'cause ya like to talk and the kid knows too much already."

"Mr. Vasquez, I can't—"

"Enrique—ya want Fuentes to pull the plug on ya?"

Enrique stood up. "Mr. Vasquez, I can't kill the kid."

"Then kick him outa here—now. Before ya do the job. And make sure the kid knows if he comes back he's dead meat—understand?"

"Yes, Mr. Vasquez."

"Bastogne's only gonna be at the farm till tonight. Madelaine's got a map for ya downstairs and an envelope with some money. Get lost. See ya in three weeks or so."

"All right—yeah," Enrique replied, and licked his lips and turned and started for the door. Behind him Vasquez reminded him about the kid.

HE COULDN'T TAKE THE GUN APART. Enrique had never asked him to, had never showed him how. "Clean it" meant wipe it with an oily rag after drying the sweat off, then, leaving the action open, use a piece of coat hanger to push a strip of rag through the barrel until it was clean and then push a piece of oily rag through the barrel. Then reload the gun.

He kept the button that held down the magazine follower wedged against the edge of the wooden table that dominated the far wall of the shed behind the house. He dropped the loose .22s one at a time into the magazine.

He hadn't shot rats with the American pistol when Enrique had given it to him—he'd shot some tin cans at ten yards or so away. He'd hit every one.

He heard the door to the shed creak open now. "You done with the gun, kid?"

It was Enrique. "*Sí*, the *pistola* is clean, Enrique."

"Gimme it," Enrique said as his huge right hand folded over the gun, his left hand snatching the magazine off the table. "Ya did good, kid. Look, ah..."

"*Sí*, Enrique?"

"The boss says you gotta split, ya know?"

"Split?"

"Get out. Ya got a mother or somethin'?"

"My mother, *cómo se, ella esta...*"

"Dead—*lo siento, amigo*—huh. Here." Enrique's hand made the Colt pistol disappear and then reappeared with a roll of American twenties. "Look, here's two hundred, go get yourself someplace to live, huh?"

"I do something bad?"

"No, kid, nothin' bad. You're a good kid," Enrique replied as his right hand rubbed through his hair again just like before, when Enrique had given him the gun. And then Enrique stuffed the money into his hands, turned around and started back to the door. A cool breeze blew through the open door.

Enrique didn't turn around, but stopped in the doorway, saying, "Be outa here, kid. Pronto, huh? Or else somebody's gonna kill ya." Enrique left.

THE KID WAS KICKING A STONE along the length of the dirt road leading down from the house. He had to do it just right because it was a big, sharp stone and he wasn't wearing shoes. He had had a pair of shoes once but someone had stolen them. Enrique had driven away in the white Ford and the kid had waved to him. Enrique hadn't waved back.

The kid kicked at the stone again, but then dodged to the side—a car was coming. He choked a little on the yellow dust cloud as the car slowed, then stopped just ahead of him.

It was Madelaine—she always threw dirty water at him, screamed at him, cursed him.

She got out of the car and stood beside the open door. "Hey kid?"

"*Sí*, Señorita Madelaine?"

He had handled Enrique's gun often enough to recognize it was a gun, but it was different from Enrique's.

"I never could stand you, ya rotten little bastard."

And then the gun went off.

2

Enrique had parked the white Ford in a field hidden from the main road by a stand of tall trees and had gone over the hill on foot. If Fuentes was in on it, Bastogne wouldn't have any guards around him.

Enrique still didn't like the idea of killing somebody's mother.

He wondered how the kid would do. And he promised himself that after he killed Bastogne and Bastogne's mother and took the three weeks in Mexico, he'd find the kid. On the streets of Ciudad Fuentes the kid would be easy enough to get hold of.

Enrique crossed through more of the trees that crowned the hilltop. The mountains in the distance were gray and cold looking—he didn't like cold things. That was the one thing he did not miss about New York—the winters. But the mountains reminded him of the tall buildings, and those memories tempered the ones of winter. He kept moving; the M-16 he carried had been handpicked by him from the latest shipment before the weapons had been sent on to Fuentes's army.

Enrique could see the farmhouse now.

He wondered why Bastogne had to be killed. He understood why Bastogne's mother would die. It was not only so she could not speak out concerning her son's murder, it was part of a program—a campaign to maintain fear, to feed the terror.

Crossed Vasquez. That was what Bastogne must have done.

Enrique thought of the kid again. The kid's mother was dead. Maybe somebody'd shot her? In the last revolution a lot of civilians had died. Maybe that was why the kid was hanging around the house in the first place looking for freebie food, why the kid slept in the toolshed with that big stick next to him to keep the rats away.

Enrique walked along the tree line, staying just far enough inside it to avoid being seen from the farmhouse.

It was a pretty neat house, Enrique thought. You could tell Bastogne had to be into something to have a house like that for his mother. Enrique admired that in Bastogne. That the Frenchman, with all his cars and all his women and the ear of General Fuentes, had remembered his mother. Taking care of your mother was a good thing to do. Enrique had sent money every week to his mother—until she died. Someday he'd go back to New York—he had promised himself that after he had sobered up—and find the punks who had knocked his mother over the head for her Social Security check. Find the punks and kill them because they had killed her.

Enrique found a good spot and kicked away some stones on the ground by the base of a tree trunk. He sat down, the rifle across his lap, a 30-round magazine in place, another 30-round magazine on the ground beside him.

An M-16 was no sniper rifle, but the distance to the farmhouse was under seventy-five yards and Bastogne would have to come out the front door to climb into the Farrari parked there. Seventy-five yards—there wasn't even any sense in using a scope. Just iron sight in—on full-auto, a couple of 3-round bursts would put Bastogne away good. And then, Enrique reminded himself, he'd have to trot down the hill and shoot Bastogne in the head a couple of times and find Bastogne's mother and kill her and then torch the house. Maybe she'd die of a heart attack when her son got shot. He hoped so. He didn't like killing somebody's mother.

Vasquez hadn't said anything about the Ferrari. Enrique considered this. He knew a man in Tapachula who would buy it, maybe pay thirty-five-thousand American for it, even though it would be a very hot car.

But Enrique couldn't drive two cars at once. If he came back for the Ferrari he would have to involve somebody else. If he took the Ferrari now, the Ford would finger him for the hit. That didn't really matter here because the cops were on Vasquez's payroll and all of them reported to General Fuentes. So he was covered.

While he solved the car problem, Enrique had been keeping an eye on the farmhouse door. Suddenly it opened.

Something about the scene temporarily jarred Enrique. It was almost as if Bastogne tripped on something and fell on his way through the doorway. And Bastogne's mother, beside him, seemed to be walking very slowly.

Enrique shrugged off the slight suspicion and turned his attention to the hit. He raised the rifle to his shoulder—he could fire from a sitting position as well as he could prone, better really since, prone, it was hard for him to cheek down on the stock at all because of his stomach. Then he lay flat.

His thumb moved the selector. It was his custom to say some words of goodbye to his victims. Usually, those were the last words the guy would ever hear. In rare situations like this where he long-distanced somebody, he felt he must honor that tradition.

"So long, Bastogne. You was good to your mother." Enrique touched his finger to the trigger. The muzzle barely climbed. Enrique had a powerful grip. He fired another 3-round burst. Bastogne, already hit, ducked behind the Ferrari. "Kiss off botherin' with the clean head shot," Enrique muttered. The third burst caught Bastogne in the chest and he went down. "Shit." He could kiss off the Ferrari, too. The windshield was blown away, and he could have sworn a couple of rounds had skipped across the hood.

The old lady just stood there, and then she did something totally inexplicable to Enrique. She broke into a dead run. "Pretty good for an old broad. *Lo siento, madre*." He touched the trigger. He put a 3-round burst square into the area between the shoulder blades, her blue dress splotching red. As the woman who had been Bastogne's mother fell to her knees in the dirt, he fired again. There was no use in making her suffer. He went for a head shot.

Bastogne's mother collapsed to the ground.

Enrique stood up and stretched, keeping the selector on full-auto just in case. He remembered to pick up the spare 30-round magazine and stuff it into his hip pocket again, then began half running, half skidding down along the hillside.

He reached the base of the hill and then started toward the house.

Enrique observed the Ferrari with sadness and then turned his attention to Bastogne's mother's body.

There was something funny about it.

He walked toward her, before going to Bastogne.

"Damn, didn't know the old lady wore no..." Her wig had fallen off, partially. It was a strange wig, its natural gray patches now matted with blood. But underneath the wig—he kicked it away—underneath, the hair was black and short. Too short.

Enrique looked toward the house, dropping to his left knee, the M-16 pistol grip tight in his right fist.

He rolled the body over. It was a young boy.

Enrique licked his lips, then stood up. It was a setup, he understood that now. He started edging back. But it was as though he was caught in some giant mechanical trap. As he backed warily toward the trees, he seemed to trip it. The shutters on the side of the farmhouse flew open.

Enrique started to shoot but there were too many for him. Soldiers. He took the hits, standing there, waiting for the one that would put him down. He thought about the kid who used to clean his gun. And about the luck that comes to a man who kills somebody's mother.

FRANÇOIS BASTOGNE walked from the house. His eyes drifted from the dead convict he had dressed in his favorite Windbreaker and sunglasses to the Ferrari. The windshield was shattered; worse than that, the hood was badly scratched. It would take time and effort to replace the hood and to match the custom shade of red. *"Merde,"* he muttered.

General Fuentes's men surrounding him, Bastogne walked toward the dead Enrique, stepping over the body of the fifteen-year-old boy to inspect the bullet holes in Enrique's body.

From the house his mother called to him, "Are you all right, François?"

"Oui, maman."

He was fine. Just fine.

VASQUEZ LOOKED AT HIS WRISTWATCH. It would be done by now.

The open briefcase was on his desk already, and he began to stuff it with the bundles of currency that he had taken from the wall safe. Hundreds, in packets of fifty. It was enough for him to retire on forever. As he was about to close the briefcase he remembered something. He walked around behind the desk and opened the top drawer. The .45 auto. He picked it out of the drawer and threw it into the briefcase on top of the money.

He had never liked guns.

Lighting a cigarette, he started for the office door.

He would have liked to have taken the collection of porno books, but he was traveling light and fast. He had to. With the money he had he could buy plenty more, Vasquez told himself.

Vasquez reached the door, turning the knob.

He started through the hallway, leaving his office door open behind him, the briefcase in his left hand, the snubby .38 special in his right hand inside his pocket.

He reached the staircase, then started down. At the base of the stairs he saw Madelaine.

"Hi, Manuel—"

"I told ya never to call me that."

"Where ya goin' with a briefcase, huh?" She was short, skinny, too broad shouldered for a woman anyhow, and she had straight red hair cut like a boy's. He had always figured she was a dyke. "Well, Manny?"

"To General Fuentes, where the hell do I usually go on Fridays, huh? And why do I usually carry a briefcase? Just shut up.'' He started down the stairs again.

Madelaine stood at the base of the stairs, unmoving. He was starting to get worried. He'd never had to shoot anybody himself; he'd always ordered it done. It was too late for that now. He might have to shoot her.

''I just got off the horn with Fuentes, Manuel. He told me you had been a bad boy. But I told the general that momma would fix everthing. Kick ass or whatever it took.''

''What the hell do you mean?'' Vasquez's right hand tightened on the gun in his pocket. He wondered if you could really shoot somebody through your coat pocket as they did in the movies.

''Sending Enrique out to croak Bastogne after tellin' Bastogne Enrique was comin'. The slob's been croaked already; Fuentes told me. And havin' me kill the kid. Who'd you have set up to kill me?''

''Look—ah—look, Madelaine. You always been square with me, huh? What I got in the briefcase—there's enough for two, ya know?''

''Better not lie. It's bad to lie just before you die, Manuel.''

Vasquez fired the revolver through his pocket and he missed. He tried again when Madelaine's gun appeared from behind her. The gun in his pocket was jammed. As he tried to pull it out of the pocket, he heard the sound of ripping cloth. The gun wouldn't budge. ''All of it, Madelaine—all of it—yours, huh? Whatchya say?''

''Drop dead, shit head.''

MADELAINE FRICKIE threw the briefcase behind the front seat of the Chevy. She had counted the money. Since she had never memorized her times tables in school, she had worked out through a complicated process that the fifty hundreds in each bundle made five thousand dollars. There were one hundred packs. She came up with a half-million dollars. Vasquez already had a plane waiting, and Fuentes would never miss the money. So, why not?

She turned the key in the ignition and started out of the driveway, off the gravel and onto the dirt, the wind ruffling her short hair. She put her foot down hard on the gas pedal. She looked on the seat beside her—her Smith and Wesson Model 39, the .45 auto she had taken from the briefcase, and the Colt Detective Special she had untangled from the pocket lining of Vasquez's suit.

Madelaine grinned.

Money.

She turned down onto the steep road that led to the highway, the dust behind her roiling in a giant yellow cloud. She looked to her right—the ditch where she had rolled the kid's body.

Enrique gone. The kid gone. Vasquez gone.

In their place, a sudden suspicion loomed up. Why had Fuentes told her about setting up Enrique and Bastogne? At the bottom of the road she stomped so hard on the brakes the Chevy began to skid, but already she was throwing the selector into reverse. A truck and two jeeps blocked the exit onto the highway.

A tall man stood at the vertex of the three vehicles, his fatigues creased so sharply they could have cut flesh, an Aussie-sytle bush hat cocked at an angle and low over his eyes. The face was handsome—like something chiseled from rock. The mustache was long, bushy, its droop accentuated by the massive cigar that hung out of the left corner of his mouth.

There was no way to take the Chevy in high-speed reverse along the dirt road and reach for one of the guns on the seat. She knew that. "Lyin' bastard," she screamed over the whine of the engine, the screech of brakes, as she stomped down hard, cutting the wheel, trying for a bootlegger turn.

The Chevy broadsided across the road. She tried giving it gas—in reverse, then in forward—but her rear wheels were over the edge of the ditch, the ditch into which she had rolled the kid.

Madelaine grabbed for the guns. The .45 in ner right hand, the Model 39 Smith in her left, the door already opened, her left foot in the dirt. The little Dick Special had fallen off the seat and she couldn't see it. She could see the briefcase but not how to take it with her.

She started to run.

Very suddenly she stopped.

She turned around. Still holding both guns, she smoothed her short red hair with the back of one hand.

Madelaine extended the guns straight ahead of her, both hammers raised.

She fired.

The tall man took the cigar from his mouth, blew gently on the glowing tip, and then casually stepped aside. The machine guns mounted in the back of the jeep fired.

She felt things tearing at her skin, abusing her flesh, felt herself being thrown back, felt...

3

Dan Track pushed his hands into the front pockets of his Levi's. He felt naked despite the jeans, cowboy boots and light blue snap-front shirt. He wore no weapons.

He chewed down on the stump of cigar in the corner of his mouth, screwing the straw cowboy hat down over his eyes as he leaned his body into the angle of the hill and walked.

Fritz Cheatum. Debbie Hinchcliffe. Lenny Dostrow. General Fuentes. Manuel "Manny" Vasquez. Some bearded semigiant named Enrique who liked to talk about New York City and killed people with a silenced .22 target pistol. The business with the Woodsman, Track could see: during World War II and afterward, silenced Colt Woodsmen had been popular Spook guns. Today there were guns better suited, but Track had respect for tradition, even in a killer. Enrique—Track shrugged it off. If the man ever came between him and Debbie Hinchcliffe, Dan Track would worry about the guy then.

Manny Vasquez. Sixty-three years old. Born in the United States—the only reason Vasquez had never been deported. Involved in the stateside drug business under the aegis of the Five Families since the middle 1950s, before that a pimp. General Fuentes...

Track took the curve through the alleyway, looking behind him once. The city, the entire country—it made his skin crawl.

And it was because of General Fuentes.

In the early 1980s Fuentes had led a military coup, theoretically Communist but in public, at least, avowedly anti-Communist. Official theory had it that Fuentes ran his right-wing army and controlled the left-wing guerrillas in order to use their atrocities as a wedge for remaining in power. Whoever won in the country, if anyone did, Fuentes would still be on top. And to power his regime and to arm his terrorists, he traded cocaine for guns and money.

Lenny Dostrow. Track considered him an idiot. Dostrow was the proverbial bad penny—bent. At age thirteen, he had murdered a Los Angeles schoolteacher. After a stint in the reformatory, he had launched his career—not murder directly, but as a middleman, selling drugs. At age twenty-eight Dostrow was in charge of overseeing the stateside end of the thriving business the crime syndicate had with General Fuentes.

All of this was the sort of thing Dan Track expected in normal life: some people were good, some people weren't and sometimes it was Track's job to get rid of those who weren't in order to protect those who were. It was logically, ethically and morally quite simple.

Track finally reached the crest of the hill. Cowboy boots were not the best choice for a mile-long walk over cobblestones. But the boots went with the hat and the shirt and the Levi's, the right costume for the identity that had been established for him. He was Pete Simpson, chief beef buyer for a large chain of supermarkets in New Mexico. Aside from exporting cocaine and revolution—the former to the United States and the latter to various portions of Central and South America—General Fuentes also exported beef. To the United States.

Track stood at the top of the hill for a moment, catching his breath. He judged the ambient temperature to be somewhere in the middle nineties; there was no breeze. He walked to his left, looking for the house numbers. It was a better neighborhood up here than at the base of the hills—the sewers ran downhill and at the base of the hill ran open in the streets at spots.

He kept walking.

The unfortunate thing was that Lenny Dostrow had taken up with a twenty-two-year-old girl named Debbie Hinchcliffe, daughter of Senator Ronald Hinchcliffe, recent appointee to Senate Intelligence Committee. Dostrow didn't know her real name. To him she was Debbie Davis.

The house numbers were going down. Track knew he had taken the proper turn.

Fernando Murphy with DEA had called and asked Dan Track, "How many times has your uncle helped you?"

"Not often enough."

"How would you like it if your uncle became very unfriendly toward you?"

"I wouldn't."

"Come and see me tomorrow afternoon. Rent a car at the airport and use the underground garage at the Smithsonian National Air and Space Museum. Meet you by the Space Capsule at four-thirty. The plane ticket's being slid under your door right now. Look for a kind of handsome Hispanic type with an aloha shirt and an unlit cigar in the left corner of his mouth."

The next day in Washington it had been raining and the handsome Hispanic had been carrying a raincoat over his arm.

The National Air and Space Museum was an interesting place for a meeting. Unless you wanted to go to a great deal of trouble, it was exceedingly difficult to get around or into any of the various museums at the Smithsonian armed—for anyone, including an undercover DEA man, unless he wanted to flash tin.

Track guessed the man hadn't wanted to do that. The aloha shirt was tucked into the Levi's and obviously didn't cover a gun.

Track had pulled on his raincoat and walked outside, following the man onto the greenbelt that to the left led toward the Washington Monument and to the right led to the Capitol. They had begun walking along the sidewalk bordering the greenbelt, toward the Capitol.

"Thanks for the airplane ticket," Track had told Fernando Murphy.

Murphy's face was dripping water. The rain was heavy.

"Hey, anytime, Track. Glad you could make it."

"Listen, anything for Uncle Sam. Maybe. What do you want?"

"DEA and some other organizations with funny letters, well, we got a problem. Thought maybe you could help us out."

Track laughed, lighting a cigar under the brim of his fedora, then walking on. "Sure—I'll get you guys some books on accounting, so you can live within your budgets."

"Fuckin' funny, Major Track."

"Mr. Track is fine."

"Okay, *Mr.* Track. Ever hear of Ronald Hinchcliffe?

"Sure. So what?"

"Hear that Senator Hinchcliffe's been named to the Senate Intelligence Committee?"

Track thought for a moment. "Something about it in *USA Today*, I think. So what? Find out he doesn't have any intelligence?"

"You're hysterical, Mr. Track."

"What's the problem with Hinchcliffe?"

Fernando Murphy stopped walking a minute, then lit his own cigar. It was already sodden and smelled like rope when it started to burn. "The senator has a daughter—Debbie. Turns out Debbie's callin' herself Debbie Davis these days. She's twenty-two. Got her ass kicked out of three eastern colleges. Was goin' to UCLA—at least the senator thought she was. Paid some dame to go to her classes under her name while she was off doin' other things."

"DEA things?" Track asked.

"Yeah," Murphy replied, nodding slowly, throwing down the cigar with evident disgust. "DEA things. Other things. She's got a boyfriend—successful young man—named Lenny Dostrow. Ever hear of him?"

"No."

"You're lucky. I have. In the import-export business. Imports coke from a very interesting little country south of Mexico. Exports U.S. currency and U.S. military weapons stolen out of west coast and southwestern states National Guard armories. Works for that group of quaint little Italian-American guys we all know and love. Hell—if I was Italian, I'd start crackin' those assholes just to redeem my name."

"Look on the bright side," Track told him, "maybe all Hispanics get blamed for Castro."

"Anyway. Little Miss Sunshine's already en route to this charming Central American neighbor of ours. With Lenny, huh? Trouble is, we think the generalissimo down there knows who she is. He puts the snatch on her, he's gotta figure he'll control Senator Hinchcliffe. Maybe he will. Doesn't know we know—neither does Hinchcliffe. But if he did control Hinchcliffe, well it would be kinda awkward. The general'd know every move we made against his drug-smuggling buddies and every move some other groups of right-thinking patriotic Americans made against the territories in Central and South America. Yes, sir, it could get *real* awkward."

"Why not pull the plug on Hinchcliffe and the committee?"

"Well, let's just say that the letter organization that came up with all this good stuff doesn't have the legal right to operate domestically, ya know? And the way they got the information, well, that was kinda illegal, too. And, well, a few other things."

"So. You want somebody to get Little Miss Sunshine back. Right?"

"Got a man down there—one of our guys. He'll help you out. But it'll be pretty much up to you. All you gotta do is put the bag on her and get her to the airport. We got a plane that'll be waitin' for you. Once you reach the airport and you're off the ground, sit back and read *Playboy* for all I care. We'll take care of her."

"And do what?"

"Give her back to her daddy with a little advice."

"If it's so simple," Track asked, "why doesn't your man there do it?"

"Can't—lot of reasons. You doin' it makes it so there's somebody to blame, for one thing. In case it goes wrong. You ready to volunteer, Mr. Track, or do you need further encouragement?"

Dan Track had "volunteered" since it seemed there was no option.

HE STOPPED WALKING NOW. The memory of Washington rain seemed to have cooled the air.

Suddenly the heat returned as he saw the house number—326.

He turned right and moved toward a narrow doorway. The door led to a walled garden. He tried the door handle—no dice. Had his life depended on it, he would have risked the barbed wire and broken bottles at the top of the wall and gone over. But it didn't—yet.

He rang the bell beside the door. It made an ominous mechanical sound like chimes wired to an alarm clock.

The sun beat down. He waited. He rang again.

He peered through the fence but could see nothing except the niches cut into the wall covered over with iron grating.

"¡Diga me!"

A woman's voice. "Hi. I'm Pete Simpson. Joe Morris asked me look you up—Joe Morris from Sante Fe?"

Dan Track didn't know if there was a Joe Morris in Santa Fe or, for that matter, if there was a meat buyer named Pete Simpson.

But the door opened.

The woman was tall and thin, her bony shoulders and upper body exposed above the neckline of the low-cut blue dress. His gaze trailed downward—she was relatively flat-chested or at least seemed to be. Where the dress stopped just below the knees, the legs—stockingless—were just as bony.

She could have been a model. He'd seen haute couture models just as skinny. The eyes—very blue despite her black hair and olive-toned skin—were compellingly beautiful. He suddenly remembered the rest of the speech he was supposed to give. "Are you Linda? Well, Joe said I'd get shot and hung out to dry if I didn't pay his respects for him. I'm Pete Simpson."

"Linda isn't my name. I'm Maria Sanchez—but Joe always called me 'Linda' as a nickname."

"It means 'pretty,' doesn't it, in Spanish?"

She visibly exhaled, then smiled.

Track laughed. "Come in, *señor*. Hurry," she urged.

Dan Track stepped through the doorway, and she slid past him, closing it behind her. "They only told me to expect a tall man with a mustache. That description fits half the men in this country, I think," she said, laughing, then wiped her right palm down along the side of her dress by the thigh and extended her hand. "I was cooking. Come inside." Track released her hand and followed her as she walked across the front garden. A fountain—not working—dominated its center. There was no grass but well-cared-for flower beds were dotted here and there.

She opened a screen door and Track followed her through into a wide, short, high-ceilinged hallway, then down three steps into a living room. From the near arm of an L-shaped brown sectional sofa, she took a huge fringed shawl, tossing it around her shoulders, hugging it to her body. "You noticed—I'm skinny." She glanced upward, shaking her brown shoulder-length hair free of the shawl. Track followed her eyes to the Casablanca-style fan that rotated almost lazily directly overhead. "With the fan—it is cool in here for me."

Track nodded, making himself smile. "Is Fritz Cheatum here?"

"Fritz is late. But he is late often. Nothing to worry about, I think. I'm fixing American food and if Fritz isn't here in five minutes, it will be ruined anyway. Why don't you eat with me, *señor*, ah, is it Simpson, really?"

"My name's Dan—Maria?"

"*Sí.* A drink?"

Track answered, "Sure."

She seemed to cocoon herself more deeply into the shawl as she walked across the room, calling over her shoulder, "Please to sit down, Dan. The couch is very comfortable."

"Thank you," Track said as he tossed his hat onto the coffee table near a collection of magazines. He started looking at them—*Vogue, Combat Handguns* and *Organic Gardening*. He suddenly noticed her shadow and he looked up. She extended a drink to him. "Thank you." He sipped it—Johnny Walker Black Label.

"Most North Americans seem to like it. It was that or white wine—that is all I drink. I keep Johnny Walker for Fritz."

"Ah..." But Track thought better of it.

"What is the matter?"

"Nothing."

"Is Fritz my lover?" She crossed around the far side of the coffee table, then dropped to her knees there on the boundary of the woven brown rug and the shining red tiled floor.

"No, that wasn't what I wanted to know," Track said, smiling.

"He is not my lover—just a friend. What was it you wished to ask?"

"Those magazines..."

"I was once a fashion model—never in *Vogue* of course, but I always wished for that. I enjoyed shooting before General Fuentes outlawed the private ownership of firearms. And I enjoy very much gardening."

Track laughed.

"What is so funny?"

"You are—but in a very nice way. You mentioned shooting...I was given to understand..."

"Sí—momentito por favor," and she was up on her feet and running across the room. Track started up. "My dinner—then your gun!" Track shook his head.

DINNER HAD BEEN FRIED CHICKEN—good—and chocolate pudding with the consistency and richness of chocolate mousse—excellent. Dan Track had forgone more Scotch in favor of a glass of Maria Sanchez's white wine, and he sipped at this now as she returned to the dining room with a wicker basket on her left arm, the shawl still wound around her upper body. Fritz Cheatum had not arrived, but she had told Track that sometimes Cheatum would be several hours late, but he always arrived eventually when he was expected.

She removed sewing from the basket—a blouse, something that looked like a slip, and a tray that held needles, thread and other related paraphernalia.

Then two guns—a three-inch-barreled Smith and Wesson revolver and a Walther P-38, both guns worn but smelling slightly of Hoppes #9 or the equivalent. "Either one that you wish, Dan."

The Smith and Wesson was a .32—a nice plinking round. But the P-38 was a fine weapon even though 9 mms weren't his favorites. Picking it up, he saw the Pl marking and realized it was once West German issue. "I was more or less hoping for a .45," Track admitted, smiling, looking at her as she knelt beside where he sat at the edge of the couch.

"Guns are very hard to smuggle in—unless you are the General Fuentes."

"Maybe I should see if he'll loan me one," Track joked, grinning.

"Sí—esta bien." Maria Sanchez, her voice a warm alto, laughed.

He had meticulously avoided the subject over dinner as she had done. But Cheatum was now very late, and there was a timetable. So Track asked her. "What's your part in all this—besides being pretty, being a good cook and keeping a sewing basket with guns in it?" He mechanically began to check the Walther. He worked the base-of-the-butt magazine release and withdrew the 8-round single-column magazine. The gun was loaded with hollowpoints. He thumbed the top round out. Federal

115-grain JHP. He stripped the rest of the rounds from the magazine as she answered him.

"I do what I think is right. I had a sister—she died. Cocaine. I contacted the DEA. They did not contact me. I do what I think is right."

"I'm sorry about your sister," Track said sincerely, not looking at her as he set the last of the eight rounds from the magazine on the table. He worked back the slide—a ninth round popped into his hand. Locking the slide back, he used his thumbnail to bounce the light from the breech end and peered through the barrel from the muzzle to inspect the bore. It was clean, almost mint.

"It was very little fired, I think. There are three spare magazines for it. I have two boxes of ammunition for it—like the ammunition there. A little less than a hundred rounds."

"How long has this magazine been loaded?"

"I keep only one magazine loaded and in the *pistola*, of course, but I rotate the magazines each week."

"Good." Track began to work down the disassembly latch. "The oil won't ruin your table, will it?"

"No—it is good for it, I think." She laughed. She had very pretty eyes and her smile was warm, her teeth even and white. "I will get you the spare magazines and the ammunition." She was on her feet again, walking barefoot now but still hugging the shawl around her. When the sun had dropped, Track, although unaccustomed to unrelenting warmth, had noticed a chill on the air.

Maria Sanchez returned just as Track began reassembly of the pistol. She set the three magazines and the two red-and-white boxes on the table beside the fourth magazine and the loose rounds from the pistol. "DEA smuggles these in to us as they can, but there are never enough for their agents and the ones who help them."

"You got a gun?" Track asked her, looking at her as she dropped to her knees on the opposite side of the table from him.

"Sí."

"What kind? I'm not shopping, just curious."

"A small one. A Beretta .25, 6.35 mm."

Track nodded. The P-38 was together again and he worked the action several times. He tested the safety. He opened the slide, then locked it and dropped a single round into the chamber, working down the stop. He sipped at his white wine, then began reloading the first magazine. "You know the operation?"

"*Sí*. To take back this North American girl—Debbie."

"Right. This will make trouble for you?"

"No. It will be all right."

Track began to load the spare magazines and Maria Sanchez began helping him. After each magazine was loaded, he slapped the butt into the palm of his hand, the spine of it hard against his flesh, to seat the rounds properly. "I don't think Cheatum's coming," he told her.

"He will come."

"Do you know where the girl is in case he doesn't."

"No. But I know where she will be *mañana por la madrugada*."

"Dawn tomorrow morning?"

"*Sí*. Because General Fuentes will be taking her there tonight and she will be there only a little time before we reach her."

"We?"

"*Sí*. She may be raped. She may need a woman."

Track shook his head. "I don't understand."

"Tonight—*esta noche—El General* will go to the airport. He will meet the girl and the man with her. Then he will kill the man."

"How do you know this?"

"I am the mistress of General Fuentes sometimes."

"Wonderful." Track smiled.

"A man—he can fight with many things. Sometimes a woman can only fight with her body, Dan."

"And her mind." Track reached out his right hand and touched her cheek.

Her lips brushed against his hand.

Then her body tensed like a spring. Track was on his feet, the safety of the P-38 up and off. The squeal of brakes. Shouts. "The general coming for a social call?"

"The general coming to kill me—quickly!" She snatched up her sandals from the floor beside the coffee table, the shawl half falling from her shoulders as she ran toward the front hallway. Track started after her, shoving the two boxes of 9 mms into the front pockets of his Levi's as he moved, his straw cowboy hat slapped onto his head. He snatched the P-38 from his belt, nearly even with her as she started toward him, a woven shoulder bag with some sort of Indian design in her hand, the sandals on her feet now.

"Where the hell are we going?"

"To escape. Hurry!"

"He'll have it guarded—"

"He never comes here! I go to him!" She ran past him toward the kitchen, Track falling in behind her, hearing the sound of the door at the wall beyond the garden being beaten down.

She was shoving aside the kitchen table. Track, beside her then, grabbed chairs, casting them aside, as well. She bent quickly, snatching up the gray woven rug that had been beneath the table. "We must hurry—the trap door!"

Track glanced along the corridor leading into the kitchen. He could hear the screen door being kicked through, shouts, curses in Spanish—some of them he didn't even understand. Track tugged hard at the ring in the trap door, finally wrenching the square of wood back on its hinges. Total darkness, like a well bottom, gaped from beyond the opening.

"You first," he told her, but she was already running, out of the kitchen through a side door. Track left the trap door open and ran after her. Maria, waiting at the doorway to the right of the kitchen, closed it as he passed through, locking it.

"Up there." She pointed to a cord that hung from what looked like another trap door. Track pulled at the cord; a drop staircase appeared and with it the smell of night air. Maria started up the ladder, pulling the shawl close around her. Track looked back once, heard gunshots from the kitchen and then climbed behind her. In seconds they stood on the roof of the house, beneath a covered portico. "Hurry! Pull the door up!"

Track handed her the P-38 and pulled at the stair frame. The stairs started to rise, Track accordioning them as the staircase slammed upward, his right foot out, breaking the momentum and stifling the echoing slam. He eased it closed and took the P-38 from her hands. She was visibly shaking in the moonlight. He didn't know if the cause was the cold or fear. It was probably both.

"We must be very quick."

Track nodded, pulling the straw Stetson low on his forehead, his eyes focused on the opening that he had just sealed. He began methodically to empty boxes of ammunition and to put the shells in the front pockets of his jeans. When he finished he folded his left arm around the woman's shoulders. She nodded, licking her lips.

They heard no more shouts from beneath the roof, but many curses.

"Now," she whispered, starting across the roof. Track followed behind her. There had been nothing to wedge into the ladder so that it would not drop. Maria Sanchez tore off the shawl, bundling it under her arm as she slung her purse to her left shoulder, then stuffing the shawl into the bag as she reached the end of the roof. She stepped out of her sandals. Track, beside her, peered over the edge. They were at the rear of the house and the hill dropped off behind them. It would be twenty feet down into darkness. Some three or four yards away there was a building—a garage or barn once—flat-roofed like the house. "The boards—we can walk across on them. Help me—*ayuda* me!"

She began trying to shift a heavy plank, Track judging its length as nearly fifteen feet. Not too gently, Track pushed her aside. The Walther went to his waistband and he wrestled the plank up, pushed it out, then levered it onto the opposite roof.

One plank in place.

Then they heard the sound of the drop ladder being pulled downward. "No time, Maria. Models learn balance. Hurry!" Track half pushed the woman up onto the ledge of the roof line, then onto the board.

Shouts, then curses. The voices were loud and a shaft of light filtered up from the room below.

Track saw a face protrude above the roof line. "*¡Alto!*"

Track drew the Walther from his waistband and worked the trigger double action, then single-actioned a second shot. There was a scream of pain as the face fell away, back down into the house.

Track stepped up to the roof ledge, then onto the board. Maria was barely visible in the darkness, but nearly across as best as he could tell. He started after her and then there was gunfire from the roof behind him. He turned and fired toward the muzzle-flashes, the board beneath his feet rocking. With effort, he regained his balance and fired, emptying the magazine. Screams pierced the darkness where the muzzle-flashes had been.

Track turned and ran the last few steps across the board walkway, jumping down onto the roof of the other building. He swapped magazines in the P-38 and kicked the board off, hearing it clatter down into the darkness.

"This way, Dan," Maria called from the shadows. Track ran toward the sound of her voice, across the roof of the smaller structure, to the far edge. "The tree—use it to climb down!" Track jumped for the notch between two large limbs, his left hand finding purchase, then his right, his legs swinging. He didn't know if it was the recommended method, but he dropped, tucking his legs under him as he hit, rolling, the hat falling from his head.

He caught the hat, whacking it clean against his thigh, reaching up as Maria Sanchez swung over him. He caught her at the hips and she let go, sinking into his arms.

"Careful. There are dogs. Follow me." She started running into the darkness, Track on her heels. There was no other choice.

Gunfire sounded from behind them but Track kept running, the loose cartridges in his jeans pockets rattling against each other. Ahead were the sounds of dogs barking. He barely avoided slamming into a wooden fence. Maria urged, "This box—stand on it." Already, she was climbing over, but Track grabbed the fence top and hauled himself up and over. Track caught Maria as she dropped.

From behind them there was a low growl. He wheeled as a dog as black as the night lunged for his throat. Track spun half right, his body angling right and down, his left leg snapping up. His foot made contact with the animal at the chest. There was a yelp, then another. Track and Maria ran again. It reminded him of being a kid in Chicago, running through backyards to get away from the cops, flippng fences, meeting angry dogs in the dark.

Another fence. There was no box to stand on this time and as Track boosted Marie up to grab the top, she panted, "We had to wait. The soldiers would have surrounded the house—but when they found the trap door, he would have called them in."

"Who? Fuentes?"

"Sí. El General."

Track caught at the fence top and flipped himself over. As he waited to guide Maria down, Track was hammered against the fence. He felt the weight of the animal and heard the snap of jaws.

Then he heard a single shot and the dog's weight went dead on him.

Track looked up. In Maria Sanchez's hand was her .25 Beretta.

Before he could thank her there was more gunfire from behind them. The ground beneath their feet dropped suddenly as they ran, angling sharply downward. "Watch out! The dirt is loose here!"

Track went into a skid, but caught himself in time, his left hand going out behind him for balance against the decline. At the base of the decline he waited for directions from Maria. In the distance he could see a darkly painted building. In the darkness punctuated only by a street lamp most detail was lost.

The woman was fumbling in her purse.

He heard the sound of keys.

"Help me with the door!" He swung open a door like those found on a barn or an old-style garage and Maria pushed past him. He heard the sound of a car door opening and closing and then saw parking lights. Track crossed to the passenger side. Track wrenched open the door of the Mustang as she leaned across and pulled up the lock, her dome light on. He slammed the door closed after him as she closed hers; there was the sound of the engine coming to life. "I expected this day. I know now why we did not see Fritz. Fuentes will have had him murdered."

"Wonderful. Not so hot for Fritz, either," Track snapped, the Mustang's engine roaring now.

Gunfire from the top of the hill. "Hold on." The Mustang lurched ahead, the headlights suddenly on, sweeping the darkness.

The car veered hard right, bouncing over something that sounded high and solid in the darkness, the headlights tracing crazy arcs in the darkness. Track peered behind them; the muzzle-flashes of the assault rifles were almost impossible to see now.

"I'm sorry for Fritz Cheatum, and you," Track told her. He knew that somehow his mission had brought it on.

"And I, Dan, I am sorry for you."

4

She opened her overnight bag and stared into the mirror set into the lid. She had fallen asleep and her hair was a mess. She took the brush from her purse and started working on her hair.

"Hey, Debbie. You look great, baby."

"I look like hell," she said, laughing, parting her hair in the middle and working the hair to both sides of it. "Anyway, I gotta look good to meet your pal the general. What's his name again?"

"Fuentes. No pal of mine." She looked across the aisle at Lenny and smiled. She had flown in enough private planes with her father that she could identify all the sounds; this one told her the landing gear was down and they were making a final approach. She gave her seat belt a final tug and closed the case, setting it in the aisle.

As she rested her hand on the top of the case to keep it from sliding forward, Lenny's hand closed over hers. "I'm glad you came with me. I really am. You aren't like any of the other girls I know—knew—"

"I heard ya the first time," Debbie quipped. Then she leaned across the aisle and kissed his cheek. "Thanks—for loving me."

"You don't thank somebody for somethin' they like to do that much, baby."

"That's not the kind of loving I mean, Len."

"I feel it, too—no shit—and it scares me." He laughed but he squeezed her hand tighter.

She looked out the window of the Beachcraft toward the ground. There were lights from some fort or city off in the distance and lights immediately ahead of them on the runway; there was only blackness in between. She looked back at Lenny, tugging at her dress a little as she asked, "Are you going to have to be with this Fuentes guy all the time?"

"No, no, we got some talkin' to do. He's been tryin' to change the arrangement's all. And he'll have us up to the palace for dinner. You ever eat in a palace before?"

He laughed, not expecting an answer, she guessed. She didn't give one. Traveling with her father, she had eaten in palaces.

The plane touched down, the tires screeching and she exhaled. Flying had always terrified her, but she had never told her father that, nor had she told Lenny.

"Okay." Lenny was already undoing his seat belt. He leaned over as he stood, ducking his head, and kissed her hard on the mouth.

Debbie laughed. "What's that for?"

"Cause I never kissed ya here before. Well, you know, in *this* country—that kinda here."

The plane seemed to taxi interminably and as she looked out the window beside her she could see other lights ahead on the otherwise darkened field. Vehicles. Latin American generals traveled with large entourages; like most dictators, they were almost pathologically afraid of being alone. When her father had been ambassador that one time—right after her mother had died—she had met her first dictator. That one wore robes and a bedouin's *keffiyeh*. This one, she imagined, wore fatigues. But underneath they would be the same.

The plane stopped.

The pilot walked back along the aisle, smiling at her. She turned her head to see as he began the door-opening ritual.

"Smile, sweetheart," Lenny encouraged.

She made herself smile, standing up, holding her overnight bag. Lenny started ahead of her along the aisle. The pilot stepped out of sight, into the night.

Lenny turned around as he stopped in the threshold of the doorway. "Hey ya know, I really do love ya," he breathed, and then started down the awkward steps. She had nearly twisted an ankle on the way into the plane. Now she waited until he was down.

Shots. The pilot fell. Lenny shouted, "Debbie!" He fell.

Debbie dropped her case; she could hear the mirror in the lid shattering.

At the base of the steps stood a man in fatigues; he was a handsome man with a big mustache and a cigar that smelled like something you stepped in by accident.

"Señorita Debbie Hinchcliffe? Welcome to my country—and I do mean *my* country."

She screamed.

5

The Mustang stopped beyond a sparsely wooded area. Maria Sanchez leaned against the steering wheel shivering as Track watched her. "What's going on, Maria?"

She began to light a cigarette, but her hands were trembling too badly and the lighter wouldn't flame. Track tumbled through the ammunition in his Levi's pocket for his Zippo. He flicked open the cowling and worked the striking wheel under his thumb, offering her the flame. She nodded, murmuring "*gracias*" through a mouthful of smoke. There was a moon now; the sky was clearing. "What is happening is something terrible, Dan."

Track picked up her cigarettes from the seat beside her, took one and lit it. "How terrible?"

"For some time Fritz had thought Fuentes was planning to take complete control of the smuggling operation. But he did not know how. I, ah, it was necessary that I renew my relationship with El General. I did this. I despise the man," she added, and made a motion with her lips as though spitting. "For a time Fuentes was a university professor in your country; perhaps this is where he knows of the senator's daughter. Or perhaps it is the criminals in your country who have told him. It is not something I know. But he knows of her identity. If he were to keep her his prisoner, he would have immense power with the Cubanos, with the Russians, with the syndicate gangsters in your country."

"Probably her father would just step down," Track murmured, inhaling on the Camel.

"What if his stepping down would cause her death?"

"He'd be forced out of office, or maybe somethin' else..."

"And if it were the something else, what sort of propaganda coup would it be?"

"A very big one," Track almost whispered. "A very big one."

"A simple exchange of data the young girl's father already knows for the assurance of her safety. It would be enough."

"The possibilities are limitless, aren't they?"

"The girl—if you cannot get her free of Fuentes—she must be killed. If you cannot do such a thing, then I will do it."

Track looked at her. "How do I get her out? Cheatum was supposed to tell me. Now he's dead. And all I know is that it's supposed to be tomorrow morning. And you know where."

"There are men and women who fight El General; they are my friends. I will take you to them. Your plane—if El General knew that Fritz had to be killed, knew that he should come to my house, he will know about this, as well."

"How then? By sea?"

"The shoreline is patrolled. You would never make it, even in the fastest craft, because helicopters are kept on the alert at all times to intercept, well, El General calls them smugglers and Communist saboteurs. But they are mostly people who would escape his tyranny, I think."

"Then how?" Track stubbed the cigarette in the dashboard ashtray between them. Their hands touched as she put out her cigarette, as well.

"The mountains—and then to Mexico. This is the only way. But first we must get her free. But you must promise that if she cannot be rescued, she will be killed."

Dan Track promised Maria Sanchez nothing.

6

"Was it hard takin' Enrique down?" Chet Halston asked Bastogne.

"But no—he walked into the trap. But my car, she was ruined. I was sitting here," Bastogne drawled, smiling, sipping at his drink, "even now wondering should I purchase a new car or attempt to have the hood replaced and then the entire vehicle repainted. And of course, the color—it is custom. A difficult decision."

Halston nodded, standing and walking toward the fireplace; the hearth was cold now and sealed with a glass cover against, he imagined, loss of the cool air-conditioned air. "I had a similar problem, François. Had a custom Lincoln Continental Town Car. Mauve, it was. The name of the color, ya know. This son of a bitch takes a shot at me, and natch, the armor plate takes care of it, but hell—you shoulda seen what a couple 9 mms did to the quarter panel. Hadda trash the car. Couldn't match that mauve color no matter what I tried; and repaints always look like repaints, ya know."

"*Mais oui*—this is true, my friend. I am very upset."

Halston just nodded, in total agreement with the Frenchman.

The doors to the study opened. He recognized the girl from seeing her with Lenny. She walked in, looking behind her, her hair in disarray, part of her dress ripped, a bruise starting to darken on her left cheekbone.

Ignacio Fuentes followed her through the open doorway, slamming the door closed behind him, a glass vase on the mantel vibrating with the force. The girl just stood there, by the doorway. Halston laughed. "Debbie, how ya doin', sweetheart?"

"You bastard." She started for him, but Fuentes caught her, spun her around and backhanded her on the right cheek. Halston thought that at least now the dame would have a matched set.

Fuentes let her fall to the floor, then stepped past her, his customary cigar in his right hand, a smile on his face. With the expression and the prop, Ignacio Fuentes looked like a nightclub stand-up comic ready to break into his act. Halston started to laugh. He could picture it now—Fuentes walking out onto the stage with six guys with M-16s; they point them at the audience and Fuentes says, "Anyone who does not laugh shall be executed immediately," then starts in with, "Ya know, a funny thing happened to me on the way here tonight."

Fuentes turned to Halston. "Señor Halston, as always, it is good to see you." He placed the cigar in his teeth and extended his right hand.

Halston took his hand and grinned. "General, I gotta hand it to ya. You and Bastogne pulled off the big one."

"It was entirely the general's leadership—inspirational," François Bastogne called from behind him.

Halston glanced over his shoulder, then back to the general's dark eyes. "We put the squeeze on her little daddy. The three of us are the most powerful men in foreign trade, huh?" Halston cracked Fuentes on the shoulder good-naturedly. Fuentes's eyes hardened above his practiced smile.

"I think some further discussion is required," Fuentes began, starting to pace the room, at trail of cigar smoke charting his path. "Further discussion of our agreement."

Halston walked back to the sofa beside the coffee table and picked up his Myers' Dark Rum and Coca-Cola. They called them Cuba Libres sometimes. He didn't like anything else about Cuba. Especially Castro. Halston was beginning to think he didn't like Latin dictators in general. "I thought it was all settled. We wanted Vasquez dead. You wanted more control. Enrique was becoming a pain in the ass to all of us."

Fuentes stopped pacing and turned on his heel. Halston could hear the girl moaning. She still lay on the floor near the doorway. "All this is true, my friends." Fuentes walked toward the bar, crossing to stand behind it. He produced a glass from beneath the bar, then reached behind him to a decanter of something that could have been gin or vodka, or even water. Fuentes began to pour, saying, "But, it is only true as far as it went." He stopped pouring, put the top back on the decanter and downed half the contents of the glass in a single swallow. "Possessing this young lady, well, it makes a very big difference, I think."

"Shit, General," Halston snapped, "you wouldn't have known who the hell she was if I hadn't—"

"Please, Señor Halston—Chet—we are all friends here."

Halston turned to Bastogne. "What do you say, François?"

The Frenchman studied his drink. "I believe, my friend, that you would be well advised to hear our dear comrade the general out on this matter." Bastogne looked away. Halston glanced once more at the girl; she was on her knees now, crying, holding her face, rocking her body like a child might rock a doll.

Halston sat down.

Fuentes downed the remainder of his drink and thumped the glass down onto the bar. "So. Controlling this young lady, I can easily force her father into imparting to me all the data he has received regarding U.S. Intelligence information in the Caribbean—everywhere. I will know exactly what the United States knows. That means—" Fuentes smiled, gesturing with his cigar toward Halston, making little circles with it in the air as he spoke "—that I will know just what the United States knows concerning our little business venture; what the United States knows concerning my noisy friend in Cuba and his ventures throughout Latin America and Africa; and what information has been learned concerning the organization you have, Chet—this Mafia—as regards smuggling and various other activities that in whole or in part are extraterritorial to the United States. I will know what countermeasures are being taken against various operations those fine fellow in the Kremlin have underway. I will know many things. Enough to cripple the overseas operations of your crime syndicate, Señor Halston—Chet. If I wish. Enough to set myself up as the most powerful exporter of cocaine in the entire world. Because with this knowledge and my association, shall we say, with the KGB, I can have the various other sources of cocaine taken over or dried up. With knowledge as my weapon, they will have no choice but cooperate. I will drive the price up. And with the guns and the money I shall receive from you or your competitors, Chet, well, I will be the most powerful force in Central America, in South America, perhaps Africa, too. She is my key—this young lady—my key to empire. The question that remains for you to answer, Chet, is simply this: do you wish to remain my friend or become my enemy? François—French are so practical—has already decided." Fuentes played with the rim of his glass, then raised his eyes. He glanced toward the girl. She was whimpering now, staring intently at nothing. "I shall take this young lady to my bed now, gentleman. Chet—let's talk some more tomorrow, huh?"

Fuentes started across the room, his cigar abandoned in the bar-top ashtray.

He stopped beside the girl. He reached his hand down to her, his fingers disappearing in the hair at the nape of her neck. Immediately, her head bent back awkwardly and she rose from her knees to her feet like a puppet. She walked—or was manoeuvered—toward the door. There was silence until the door slammed behind them.

Halston didn't care if the room was wired. He looked at Bastogne. "He's fuckin' crazy."

Bastogne shrugged. "That is probably true, but he holds the power as surely as he held that girl. And it is his game now, isn't it?"

"You just gonna sit there—all the action you got goin' for you in Europe?"

"Precisely. Otherwise, it shall all be his action and if he does not kill me, my own people will. You might consider this yourself, *mon ami*. If we work with him, we shall both be very rich. If we do not, we shall be very dead, I think. I have made my decision." He raised his glass as though offering a toast. "To our new leader."

Halston stared sickly at his Cuba Libre.

HER NECK WAS CRAMPING, her head ached, her nose was dripping, her dress was ripped and she was crying. He stopped walking her down the corridor and threw open a large door, then shoved her inside. She fell to her knees, then to her face. At least the pressure of his hand against her neck, in her hair, was gone now.

On her hands and knees she looked toward the doorway.

Fuentes slammed the door, then began to unbutton his shirt. He was incredibly handsome, incredibly evil, she thought. She hadn't known about Lenny smuggling drugs. She thought he smuggled guns in exchange for money. She had always thought it ironic, oddly appealing. Steal guns from her father's war-mongering country and give them to the poor people of Latin America so they could rise up and force their governments to crumple. There were so many poor, so many starving, so many illiterate. So few rich who had it all and oppressed the people whose toil had made the rich even richer. She had liked what Lenny was doing. At least, she thought so then.

Fuentes had been a revolutionary, but he was a drug smuggler. If he didn't kill her, her father would.

Fuentes stripped off his shirt and threw it to the floor. "Crawl over here." He perched himself at the edge of a writing desk. "Take off my boots."

She sniffed back a tear, looking at him. Fuentes tugged the wide black leather belt from his trousers, doubled it, then crossed the room to her in two strides. The belt snapped downward. She screamed at the pain across her shoulders.

He returned to his perch against the edge of the desk. "Crawl over here."

She started toward him, on her hands and knees.

After a moment she knelt before his feet.

Fuentes said nothing.

She began to untie his boots.

7

A fan moved overhead, not lazily like the fan in Maria Sanchez's house, but with a jerky, frenetic movement. Track sat in the corner on a wicker-bottomed kitchen chair, well out of range of the fan's blades should the fan pick this precise moment to detach itself from the ceiling. The cowboy hat low over his eyes, a cigar, unlit, clamped in his teeth, he watched, listened, said nothing.

Beneath the fan, Maria Sanchez sat on a bar stool at a round, seen-better-days green-felt-covered table. The stool made her seem almost ridiculously fragile, like something set on a pedestal. But she was not the sort of woman one would normally place on a pedestal, Track thought absently. As she admitted, she had used her body to get information. But perhaps that set her above someone who valued traditional morality above truth.

Mentally, Dan Track shrugged.

He could follow what they said reasonably well, although sometimes the Spanish was too rapid or too sloppily pronounced to catch. Maria Sanchez was emphasizing certain facts—that Generalissimo Ignacio Jose Fuentes would be so all powerful if he used the girl to extort information from her father that he could never be defeated. That Fuentes was so confident of his own position and the lack of will among his country's people that he would commit any atrocity. That the cocaine he smuggled out of his country and into the United States was in itself an unspeakable evil. That Fuentes was very close to being the devil and should be killed.

Track had never met the man. He hoped he never would.

The conversation eddied and flowed from one point to the next and back again, rising and falling in intensity, more a study in wave motion than group dynamics.

Track finally lit the cigar and stood, deciding it was better to risk the perils of an improperly mounted ceiling fan than risk dying of boredom from the conversation that seemed to be going nowhere. He glanced at the black-faced Rolex Sea Dweller on his left wrist—time was running out. It would be dawn before long.

The four leaders of what Maria had called the Resistance turned from her and faced him. Resistance to what, Track thought—to the right wing that Fuentes ostensibly represented or to the left wing that Fuentes nurtured? "I speak Spanish," Dan Track began, "but I don't speak it well enough for this." He turned to Maria—her English seemed almost too perfect; perhaps it went with the blue eyes somehow, he thought. "Can you translate?"

"There is no need. Julio attended the university in Florida. Jésus was part of the embassy staff of our country in Washington before the coup of El

General. Martin—his dead wife was North American. And Phillipe was the chauffeur for the United States consul until the terrorists killed the consul's brother and the consul was transferred from here. He was a good friend to Fritz Cheatum."

"Fine," Track said, nodding. He turned away from the table, then in one wide stride caught up his chair, boosting it up and setting it down between Maria and the one she had identified as Phillipe. Twisting the chair forward, Track straddled the seat. "I was sent down here for one reason—to get the girl. And it looks like if I don't get the girl she's going to cause you a lot of problems and cause my country a lot of problems, as well. Maria suggested earlier that if for some reason we can't free Debbie, then we should kill her. I'm not about to murder the daughter of a United States senator or let anyone else do it, either. Killing her wouldn't do any of us any good anyway. If we find ourselves in such a hopeless position that we can't get the girl out alive, we're not going to be able to get her body out, either—which means this Fuentes and his people could still work on the senator by insisting that she is alive. If Fuentes has KGB contacts, he has some pretty good photographic and technical skills available to him. And if we kill her, Fuentes has a propaganda tool that he can milk in the press all over the world—'U.S. Assassin Murders U.S. Senator's Daughter in Underdeveloped Latin American Nation'—crap like that. As long as he has the girl, or if we kill her, Fuentes controls the ball game. If we get the girl—alive—and get her out of the country to safety, Fuetnes is up shit creek without a paddle. That's the only way. I can't do it without your help. The airport will be cut off to me. I can't use the seacoast I've been told. Means I have to take her cross-country, and Fuentes will be behind us every step of the way. I can handle that—I don't want to, but I can. I can't handle getting her out of the presidential palace all alone. For that I need help, even if it's only information. That means I need you guys.'' Track flicked the ashes from his cigar into the ashtray at the center of the table. ''So what about it?''

It was the one named Jésus who spoke. ''Your logic, *señor*—it is irrefutable. I shall get the charts for the palace at once.''

8

There was a strange power about him. He was cruel. He was demanding. He abused her. But he had made her body feel more alive than it had ever felt. She ached with the guilty pleasure of it. He had slept—for what in her own sleepless state she had judged as hours, but perhaps it was only minutes. And then he had come to her again and she had screamed—with the pain at first, and then with the pleasure his brutality gave her. Hands that had first dug into his body to give him pain now kneaded his flesh to give him pleasure.

It was her body's betrayal that made her despise herself. She did not want him to stop—ever. "I need you," she had whispered into the ear of Ignacio Fuentes as he slammed his body against hers.

And she had felt self-loathing and disgust, but pleasure, too, as he murmured, his breath hot against her face, his lips touching her eyelids, "I know that you do, *niña*."

IT HAD NOT TAKEN TRACK LONG to assess the situation. In the basement of the old church that was used as a headquarters by the Resistance to El General, they had carefully studied the plans of the presidential palace. Jésus, who under the previous administration had spent considerable time in the palace and around its grounds, had answered in detail every question Track had asked.

Track had inventoried the equipment. No SPAS 12 police shotgun, no Metalife Custom L-Frame, no Trapper Scorpion .45. Of the available weapons the Resistance had offered, there had been nothing he cared to substitute for the Walther P-38 he had been given by Maria Sanchez. He supplemented it with a Fazendeiro, one of the Brazilian knives of stainless steel and impressive proportions, the lock-blade folder identical to one he had left behind him in the States. The Resistance had no submachine guns, but he had picked the best of the twice-stolen M-16 rifles—stolen first by the smugglers who had brought them into the hands of Fuentes and then stolen a second time by the Resistance. The Resistance, Track had realized early on, was caught in the middle. Identified by the foreign press, based on Fuentes's propaganda, as an arm of the terrorist Communist guerrillas, they were in fact representative of a great many political beliefs. But they supported neither the Communist terrorists nor the fake right-wing movement of Fuentes. They were hunted by both sides with equal ferocity and had, as Track objectively assessed it, a snowball's chance in hell of success.

He would enter the facility alone. Added numbers would have been an advantage but the personnel of the Resistance were not trained in stealth and penetration techniques. Over the years Track had trained himself.

After loading six magazines for the M-16—each a thirty-rounder—he pulled on the dark blue crew-neck sweater Martin had sent him over the cowboy shirt he had worn through the day. He was hot in the sweater, but he needed darker clothing and nothing with shiny, noisy snaps to scratch on wall surfaces.

Phillipe carried a Luger in a Bianchi X-15 shoulder holster that Track had commandeered for the P-38. Slipping the holster harness across his shoulders and securing the base at his belt, Track picked up his cigar. It hadn't gone out, and he inhaled on it heavily.

It might be his last smoke.

The Fazendeiro was in his right hip pocket. The spare magazines for the P-38 were secreted about him in pants and shirt pockets.

He didn't feel ready, but he had no choice.

9

Dan Track stepped out of the station wagon. The night was warm, too warm for all the clothes that he wore. He stripped away the borrowed Windbreaker that had covered the shoulder holster and threw it on the front seat. His straw cowboy hat was on the back seat.

Track walked around to the front of the station wagon, staring down in the darkness toward the sound of the rushing water. Maria got out of the driver's side, her shawl tightly about her, and began to speak. "The stream runs its course from the base of the mountain. You will be walking against the flow. Then follow the stream toward the cavern until you reach the chimney of rock. There you will start to climb up."

Dan Track looked at her. "The bats around here vampires?"

"Yes but they will rarely attack a human."

"Rabid?"

"Most likely, yes. There is that possibility."

Track nodded. He walked toward Maria. "You just be waiting here when Debbie and I get out." He glanced at the Rolex on his left wrist, then rolled the sweater cuff back over it. "If I'm not here by 7:00 A.M., get the hell out."

"How much leeway?"

"None. If I can't get here by 7:00, I'll make my own way to the rendezvous. You wait too long, they're gonna get you."

"Agreed." Maria leaned over and planted a kiss full on Track's mouth. "*Suerte*—for luck, as you say."

"Suerte," Track whispered. He reached for the M-16 from beneath the blanket on the back seat and with it the green gas-mask bag that carried the five spare magazines. He slung the gas-mask bag to his left side, the M-16 to his right, cross body, then looked at Maria again. *"Suerte,"* he repeated, and started down the gently inclined ravine—toward the sound of the water.

The angle of the ravine steepened suddenly as Jésus had warned that it would. As Track skidded and slid downward, he began again to review the other details Jésus supplied. The presidential palace was built at the end of the nineteenth century. Then, as now, it had been more practical for prisoners taken for questioning to the palace never to leave it alive. For that reason, the guard room had been built over a chimney of rock covered with a trap door. A body thrown down the chimney would be caught by the current and swept away, only to be discovered by some peasant miles away from the palace.

Track reached the stream—maybe he could expense the ruined cowboy boots, he thought. He stepped into the water and hugged the bank as he moved against the current, the water level just below his crotch.

The thing with the guard room and the trap door leading to watery death beneath reminded Track of Douglas Fairbanks Jr. threatening one of Ronald Colman's alter egos in *The Prisoner of Zenda*. Track had read the novel by Anthony Hope and had seen various versions of it on the screen, but he had never imagined that he would be faced with a duplicate of the set.

The water was getting deeper; he carried the M-16 at chest level now. He made a mental note to kick the crap out of the DEA man who had gotten him into this. Assuming he got out of it.

He slogged ahead.

The idea of bats distressed him. Like most human beings, he felt there was something about the rodentlike creatures; which summoned up childhood terrors. He dredged his memory for bat lore. At night the bats would be out hunting or sucking on penned livestock or something. But by morning they would be returning. By morning, he would be dragging a frightened girl against the tide of bloodsucking, rabid bats—and that was the good news. There was a considerable distance to go yet. Dan Track kept walking.

THE SOUND OF THE RUSHING WATER was somehow different now. Track slowed in the chest-deep water. The bottom of the Bianchi X-15 rig and the gas-mask bag with the spare magazines were wet. But there was no way around it.

The stream narrowed, white water flecking the blackness. Track sagged his weight against the wrought-iron grillwork. The bars were massive—as he had been told they would be.

He glanced into the darkness behind him. Nothing.

Track stopped, the water to his chin now, his weapons completely immersed, and felt for the base of the bars. He thought he had it, but in the almost total darkness, there was no way to tell for certain.

He looked right and left again, then behind him, cinching the M-16 tighter against his chest. Then he began to fill his lungs. He would be fighting the current that had become swift in the narrows. There was no telling how much sediment would have collected at the base of the grate over the eighty-some years since it had been installed. Or how much of anything else.

He was ready now. He took the final breath, then tucked quickly beneath the water. Totally sightless, he had to rely on his gloved hands to follow the shapes of the grillwork downward, groping when there appeared to be an opening. He was still holding his breath easily enough. Suddenly an alarm went off in his brain. The shape he felt—there was something familiar yet horrible about it. It was a human skull. He set it aside as gently as he could, and then his hands shoveled back silt and felt like more bones. His heart was becoming increasingly more audible to him now; his lungs were beginning to ache. He was just about to surface when his hands dislodged a large slab of rock.

Mentally Dan Track said, the hell with it, and dragged himself downward, starting beneath the grating. As he inched beneath it, his sweater caught and tugged it clear. The sling—it was caught. He reached behind him, the current tearing at his face, his lungs burning now, the noise of the current drowned out by the hammering of his heart. He was starting to lose it, to feel light-headed.

He tugged at the sling, twisting on his chest, ramming himself beneath the grate. His arm flailed, his hands clawing him toward the surface. His head broke water and he gulped air coughing, vomiting water. He shook his head to clear it, his eyes burning as he coughed. Rolling back the sodden cuff of the sweater, he read the luminous black face of the Rolex nearly six. He swam now, along the course of the stream, the tunnel surrounding him on all sides but visible only when an occasional shaft of light from the tunnel mouth caught a glistening outcrop of rock.

THE WATER LEVEL HAD DROPPED, and now Track, the sweater drooping to his crotch, his cowboy boots recently flushed of the water they had taken on, walked ahead in total darkness, his right hand feeling out along the wall surface.

The important thing was not to miss the chimney going upward. The niche for the chimney started along this wall, but how far along he could not tell. Jésus had never traversed the tunnel; he had only read in the blueprints of the structure about the tunnel's design and had known of its hideous purpose. As Track had left the man, Jésus had cautioned, "*Señor*, it is possible that El General has had the chimney sealed. If this is so, then all—it is lost.

Track kept moving. So far there had been no bats, but he knew where they would congregate—in the chimney itself. Track stopped—the niche of rock. He felt it, both hands going out in the darkness. He felt along it vertically, finding the top of the niche, lintellike—then tracing along this laterally until he found the opposite side. The dimensions seemed to match. With his right foot, his hands balanced against the sides of the niche, he explored for the base. It seemed like a step. Carefully, because he knew it would be slippery, Track raised his right leg into the niche, moving his foot to get a secure purchase. He gulped air, then crawled inside the niche, rather than risk a fall climbing into it conventionally. He moved along for what he judged to be several feet, then raised his head taking in air. Track pushed himself up gradually to avoid knocking his head. A wise decision. He felt above him; the ceiling of the niche of rock was low, too low for him to stand fully erect. Shaking water from the muzzle of the M-16, he moved ahead along the small tunnel within the niche, feeling along the ceiling line of the wall for another opening. He found it and stopped.

There was no way to know in advance if, when he reached the height of the chimney, the trap door would still be functional. Perhaps it was sealed. Perhaps some heavy object had been placed over it. But Phillipe had conjectured that political prisoners were still thrown to their deaths here, weighted down. Twice, bodies had been found, the heads swathed in shredded plastic trash bags, the hands and ankles bound, the feet weighted down with rocks and chains.

Dan Track started to climb along the height of the chimney, finding the rough-textured, iron hand and foot rungs, the M-16 slung across his back, his clothes dripping water.

Upward, into the darkness.

Suddenly Track squinted his eyes shut; blindingly brilliant light flooding down on him and with it the sound of a muffled scream. As he opened his eyes against the light, an object—he couldn't be sure what—hurtled downward past him. His footing gone, Track swung from one of the rungs by his clenched right fist.

There was a clanging sound above him and the light died. In contrast the blackness seemed more intense.

Beneath him, in the darkness, Track heard muffled cries. He started downward, by feel, careful of his footing, until his right foot touched something that gave.

He stepped down, hearing muffled gurgling sounds now. He dropped to his knees and his hands groped in the darkness. Human legs, chains bound around them. He reached out along the length of the legs, his hands stopping as he found a trouser band. Then he wrenched the thrashing body toward him.

His hands moved along the chest, then to the head where a plastic bag fitted like a second skin.

Track's gloved hands tore at it and the gurgling sounds got louder.

The Fazendeiro—his right hand found the knife in the front pocket of his Levi's and he one-handed it open, cautious lest he kill the human being he was trying to save. He slit the bag along the crown of the skull as gently as possible, then clapped the knife into his teeth by the handle slabs and tore at the bag. Out of it came coughing, sputtering, a murmured, "*Madre de Dios.*"

"Get your breath. I'm a friend," Track declared through clenched teeth.

The voice came back from the dark, still coughing. "You have saved me."

"Not quite yet. Let me try to get those chains off."

"They are knotted only; they do not waste their stolen money on a lock for such as me."

"You all right otherwise?" Track asked, finding the knot by feel, beginning to pry the links free.

"*Si, esta bien.* I am alive. That is important—the most important thing now."

He mastered the knot and began to unwrap the chain from the man's ankles. Under the chain he discovered rope.

He took the Fazendeiro from between his teeth and cut by feel in the darkness. "Don't move around. I don't wanna cut your ankles."

"My wrists, also, *señor*. Who are you?"

"City inspector. I'm checking out all these old tunnels for bodies. They clog up the pipes. There. Now, sit up."

Track could hear the sounds of plastic ripping. The man must be tearing from around his neck. "What did you do to get thrown down here?" Track asked.

"I spoke for freedom. I spoke against El General's smuggling of cocaine. I am—was—a professor at the university."

Track licked his lips, glancing upward toward the darkness. "You've got a choice," Track whispered. "What's your name anyway?"

"Soy Pedro de Santiago Vargas."

"Señor Vargas, you can either go along this tunnel alone—I can tell you how—or you can wait until I come back. If you chose the latter you might never get out."

"You go inside?"

"Yes. There's a woman. I don't know where she's being held but I have to get her out. Are there any more prisoners?"

"*Sí.* There are many. Eighteen men, perhaps twenty. Five women—the women can be heard at night, when the guards take their liberties with them. But you were wrong, *señor*. There is, I think, the third alternative. I believe in freedom. I can go with you. I have my hands to fight."

It was insanity. In total darkness, Track had no idea of the man's age. But there was a certain strength, a certain resolve in the voice. "How old are you Señor Vargas?"

"I have fifty-eight years, *señor*. But before I was arrested, I would run each day. I swim. I served in my country's army when I was young—"

"All right. Here." Track reached to the P-38 under his armpit, the X-15 rig wet still, the pistol doomed to rust, he knew. He shook the pistol, "Push the safety up when you want to fire. Eight rounds in the magazine, one in the chamber. Just pull the trigger. The first shot'll be double action." Track found the man's hands in the dark and pressed the P-38 between the man's splayed fingers. "Can you use it?"

"*Sí*. I can use it. It feels like a Luger."

"It's a P-38. Lot's better. Come on. There are rungs. Let me take your hand and show you." Track took Vargas's left hand, guiding it toward the wall where the rungs were located. "We'll free them all. Or we won't free any of them. When we make it up, kill somebody and take an assault rifle, and don't forget to grab some spare magazines. Keep the pistol I gave you in your trouser pocket while we climb. If you put it in your waistband it could slip out. The trap door," Track began as he climbed, "how is it positioned in relation to the guards? Is anything kept over it? Tell me quickly now." Track could hear the scratching sounds of Vargas moving along beneath him as they climbed.

"There is a—what is your word—a desk. The trap door is three meters from the desk. Behind the desk sits a guard. He carries only a pistol. The room where the guards rest when they do not make interrogations or patrol the cell block—it is beyond the trap door, which is behind the desk, *señor*. What is your name—how are you called?"

"Dan Track."

"My amigos, they call me Pedro, *señor*.

"My amigos call me Dan," Track whispered back. "Pedro. We must be silent now. We'll push back the door and start killing. Do you understand?"

"*Sí*—this I understand."

"All right." Track continued upward, the M-16 suspended on its sling across his back, and as he raised his left arm toward the rung above, he could see the face of the Rolex. It was almost six-thirty.

10

Dan Track pushed his hand very gently against the trap door, his eyes squinting to prevent the light from above temporarily blinding him. Pedro, beneath him on the iron rungs, whispered, "I am ready, Dan."

When his eyelids had adjusted, Track threw his weight against the trap door. As it flew back, he catapulted through it. On his knees on the guardroom floor beside the trap door, Track fired a burst with the M-16 and killed the man who rose from behind the desk.

On his feet now, Track started to run, flipping the desk, the papers, the blotter, the pencils, all of the things on top of the desk falling to the floor as he hit the other side.

A doorway led into the "lounge" the guards used between beatings and torture sessions. Track aimed a double tae kwon do kick at the door; the lock plate sprung and the door flew inward. He completed the rotation, both feet firmly planted now as he framed himself in the doorway. "Eat lead, bastards," Track rasped, firing. There were six men. Track's first 3-round burst cut into the nearest man to the doorway, tearing into his throat and face.

One of the guards was sitting bolt upright on a cot in the far corner, a pistol in his hands, Track pumped the 3-round burst into his chest. Track stepped as a burst of gunfire from an M-16 in the far corner of the room ripped chunks out of the door frame. Track fired, all three of his shots impacting the guard in the abdomen. The man's body jackknifed, hurtling back into a fourth guard. As the fourth guard pushed the dead man away, Track fired, killing him. Track wheeled left, spaying the last two men as they charged for him.

Track dropped to his knees beside a wooden chest and threw open the lid—loaded magazines for M-16s, thirties, all of them. He dumped the nearly spent magazine from his rifle and replaced it with one of the fresh ones from the chest. Thirty in the magazine, one in the chamber now.

Track grabbed more of the fresh magazines, ramming them into his waistband under his sweater, and tossed Pedro an M-16.

"*¡Ah, muy bien, señor!*"

Track nodded and handed him six magazines. Pedro handed back the P-38. "Let's check out those prisoners. Lead the way."

Pedro headed down a passageway flanking the guardroom on the right. Track followed, scanning each niche in the stone corridor's walls with the muzzle of the M-16. Randomly placed window-size doors seemingly led nowhere.

Then, the cells—he could smell them before he could see them.

Pedro skidded to a halt as the passageway opened onto six cells.

And for the first time Track actually registered Pedro's appearance. Like the men and few women in the cells, Pedro was dressed in stained rags. His face was gaunt, unshaven and his hair was greasy. There were bruises on his face and arms, and where the shirt Pedro wore was ripped down the center of the back, Track could see lash marks.

"¿Donde estan los Uaves?"

"Aquí," Pedro answered. Track nodded as Pedro ran to a peg on the wall just out of reach of the nearest cell. The psychological torture—of the keys in sight but unreachable.

Track could hear the sounds of the key turning in each lock in succession, but there was still no movement from the far end of the passageway. He could hear crying, laughter—the sounds of freedom. Without looking back Track called to Pedro, "Get 'em up along the passageway. Hurry!"

Track ran to the end of the passageway—no activity. He returned to the guardroom to scrounge weapons. Five M-16s, three 1911A1s—he liked the .45 better than any 9 mm, but as-issued government pistols weren't noted for their accuracy.

He threw the three pistols, the spare magazines for them, two knives and a bayonet into the wooden chest and then dragged it out of the guard lounge and beyond the desk just outside.

He returned to the room, grabbing the five M-16s, then ran back through the doorway, hearing the sounds of Pedro coming with the freed prisoners.

"Pedro, any of them ready to fight?"

"*Sí*, Dan."

"Issue weapons to the fighters—pick five men. Send the rest of the weapons and the rest of the prisoners down the chimney and into the stream. Tell them when they leave the niche, turn left, follow the current. At the point where the stream leaves the mountain there's a grating. All they need to do is hold their breath and crawl under the grating and they're free. Anyone who can't swim, have 'em stick with someone who can. You coming?"

"With you—*señor*!"

"I'm starting now. Catch up with me." Track broke for the stairs at the far end of the guard complex, taking them three at a time in a run. While Jésus had gone over the plans of the presidential palace with him, Maria Sanchez had outlined El General's personal habits. Any new female prisoner would spend her first night in El General's bed, unless she was too old or ugly. Track reached a landing, swung around it and into the next flight. El General fancied himself a Don Juan, but he enjoyed brutalizing the women, as well, Maria had said. Track reached another landing, hearing sounds of footsteps above him. There was no time for a cat-and-mouse game on the stairs. Track swung past the second landing and into the stairwell, the M-16's muzzle coming on line. Two uniformed guards appeared, laughing. Track shot them dead.

He ran the stairs now, stopping beside the nearest body. Beside it was an M-16, no spare magazines. Mechanically Track checked the magazine—it seemed fully loaded. Reinserting it up the well, Track worked the bolt, leaving the selector on auto. There was another M-16 beside the second body. He disentangled it from the dead man, then propped it against the banister. Pedro or one of the others could use it.

Track started upward again, stopping at a doorway on the final landing. If the gunfire had been heard, there would be armed personnel waiting on the other side.

He shrugged, turning the doorknob slowly, then throwing the door open.

An M-16 in each hand, Track ran through the door and skidded to his knees just beyond it. To the left—three armed men. Track dropped to his right side and elbow, the M-16 in his left fist spitting death. He rolled, the floor beside him chewing up under assault-rifle fire. Prone now, an M-16 in each hand, Track fired, cutting down the remaining two of the three men.

The M-16s thrust ahead of him, he started to run. He was in what appeared to be the living quarters for the guards. He could smell food as he passed steel double swinging doors. He kept running to a stairway at the far end.

He stopped at the base of the stairway, swapping to a full magazine in first one, then the second M-16. He looked behind him.

Pedro and the others were coming, four men and a girl with him, the girl stopping to search the bodies of the three dead men. She handed off two of the M-16s, took one for herself, then ran after the others. Track judged her to be no more than sixteen.

Pedro stopped beside Track at the base of the stairs. "We are ready, Dan. The living quarters upstairs—if the guards there heard the gunfire..."

"I know," Track said. "Follow me!" He slowly climbed the stairs, the M-16s ahead of him.

11

Chet Halston knew gunfire when he heard it.

He had heard it coming from below and followed by the sound of running in the hallway.

Frantically he was pulling on his clothes.

What was happening mattered little to him. If he could use it as an excuse to leave the presidential palace, he was all for it.

He shrugged into his shirt and zipped his fly. As he stuffed his sockless feet into his Gucci loafers, he reached to the nightstand for the Bianchi 9R shoulder rig and the 66 2 1/2 Smith. He shrugged into the shoulder rig as he started for the door; the elastic crossover strap was twisted but he didn't take the time to straighten it. He grabbed his attaché case—his business papers, a change of socks, underwear and shirt and spare ammo for the Smith and Wesson—and caught up his jacket.

Halston stopped at the door of his suite.

Bastogne had gone over. Bastogne was crazy.

Fuentes was dangerously insane. Halston knew the crazy ones could be useful, but that they were always dangerous.

He slipped on his jacket, his attaché case in his left hand, and opened the door inward. Then his right hand moved under his coat, his fist closing on the smallish grip of the .357 Magnum as he stepped into the hallway. Three uniformed presidential guards raced past him, Halston dodging back to avoid getting knocked over. He followed the guards along the upstairs hallway and toward the circular staircase.

He looked back once toward the suite at the far end of the hallway, where Fuentes's quarters were. If Fuentes wasn't up, leading his troops, this senator's daughter must be something.

As Halston reached the top of the stairs, he heard automatic weapons fire from the rear of the house. He started down, taking the stairs two at a time, his hand never leaving the .357.

The gunfire was becoming more sporadic.

Halston reached the base of the stairs and glanced toward the rear of the house. A man in dark blue clothing with an M-16 in each hand was running along the corridor, toward the front of the house. Trailing behind him were five men and a woman dressed in rags.

Halston started to run toward the front door.

He recognized the two uniformed guards who stood beside the doorway. They spoke English, not well but adequately. "More of the terrorists have gotten in upstairs. El General's fighting them bravely."

"I will go." The nearer of the two men ran for the staircase, taking the stairs three at a time in a headlong lunge.

"You'd better go, too," Halston urged the second guard.

"I must stay at my post, Señor Halston."

"Right." Halston nodded, turning away, the 66 snapping out of the leather. He wheeled back and pumped two shots into the guard's abdomen and chest.

As the guard fell back, Halston reached for the door handle, twisting it, his attaché case under his arm now. He stepped outside: no gunfire here, only the sounds of vehicles revving and shouted commands.

Halston raced down the steps and into the courtyard. Guards were everywhere. "El General—he needs you inside," Halston shouted to anyone who would listen. Some of the guards ran for the front doorway.

A jeep. Halston ran toward it; a man in fatigues and wearing a .45 in a tanker-style chest holster sat behind the wheel. As he ran, he looked to his right—the gates to the courtyard were open.

Halston stopped beside the jeep. The driver started to turn toward him. Halston brought the 66 2 1/2 from behind his back and fired twice into the driver's face.

The body slumped across the wheel, blood spurting from the eye-socket-like wounds in the forehead and left cheek. Halston jumped up beside the dead man, rolled the body out of the jeep onto the courtyard floor and fired the ignition.

He stomped the clutch, skipping first and hauling the stick into second as he cut the wheel into a hard left, releasing the clutch. The jeep lurched, and sputtered, but started ahead. A guard beside the open gates raised his right hand as a signal to halt. Halston pushed the 66 over the turned-down windshield of the jeep and fired, the guard falling back, his hands grasping toward his chest. Halston upshifted into third, cutting the wheel right. The jeep bounced over the body of the guard as Halston cleared the gates.

His smugglers would be loyal to him. Fuentes gave them abuse—but he gave them money.

Temporarily reassured, Halston hit the gas pedal.

12

Dan Track started up the circular staircase, Pedro and the others behind him. Halfway to the top he paused to pump lead into the guard who blocked the way, emptying both partially spent magazines into the body. Track sidestepped it, dumping the empty magazines and reloading.

The stairs opened onto a long corridor, reaching toward the back of the house. Fuentes's quarters should be there. So should the girl.

He shouted to Pedro, "Leave two men at the head of the stairs and check each of the rooms as you go by!" The doors at the far end of the corridor opened with a blaze of pistol shots, and a chunk of plaster in the wall to Track's left exploded outward. Track returned the fire, shooting high, splintering the lintel above the doors. The doors slammed shut.

He guessed he had just traded shots with Fuentes. Track flattened himself beside the double doors. From behind them came the sound of glass breaking. Track stepped away from the wall, spun around and split open the doors with a double tai kwon do kick. As Track started to throw himself through the opening, Pedro ran past him, shouting in Spanish, "I shall kill you!"

Assault-rifle fire was followed by the dull thudding blast of a pistol.

Track was through the doorway.

The doors to the balcony were shattered. Draped over the balcony railing was a nearly naked body, and lying on the floor at the foot of the king-size bed was Pedro. Track glanced toward the bed for an instant; in it, a blond girl naked from the waist up, her lower body covered by a sheet, was screaming.

Track kicked through the broken glass; the doors to the balcony were locked, he realized, and someone hadn't had time to find the key. Track moved to the body draped over the balcony railing. He recognized the face from the newspaper photographs and from the description given him by Maria Sanchez. It was Ignacio Fuentes. The body twitched; he was still breathing. Track looked back into the suite. Pedro was obviously dead. The girl—Debbie—had bruises on her face and breasts. Track turned back to Fuentes. He pulled the trigger of the M-16, pumping a 3-round burst into the head, then dropped the rifle to his side, grabbing the body by the hands and forearms and thrusting it over the balcony railing to the courtyard below.

Guards moved about the courtyard; there were vehicles everywhere. The body crashed through the roof of a van fitted with light bars across the roof line.

Track ran back toward the bed; the girl was still screaming. He knelt beside the fallen Pedro and rolled the body over, murmuring, *"Adios, amigo."* He thumbed down the luckless man's eyelids.

Track stood and stared at the girl. She had stopped screaming incoherently and was shouting instead. "Murderer! Murderer!"

Track knelt on the base of the bed and edged toward her. "He kidnapped you. What'd he do—kill your boyfriend? Then he hauls you up to his room. He beat you, right? And he raped you? And *I'm* a murderer?"

"I loved him."

There was no time to explain the psychology of captives to her. Track's right fist hammered out, crossing the girl at the tip of the jaw, his left hand catching at her right shoulder to keep her head from cracking back against the elaborately carved headboard.

There would have to be a change of plan, he thought. He could get a frightened or grateful Debbie through the river currents and the bats. Even a dead Debbie would have been manageable. But a vengeful Debbie who had fallen in love with the tormentor he had killed was out of the question.

The sound of gunfire came from the base of the stairs, but there was no fighting on this floor that he could detect. He dragged the girl's unconscious form to the center of the bed, rolling her body in the top sheet. He sat the girl up, then shouldered into her abdomen, slinging her across his back in a modified fireman's carry. He grabbed one of the M-16s and started toward the door.

In the hallway the young female prisoner and two of the males waited.

"Pedro is dead," he told the girl. "We're getting out of here. Not the way we came. Into the courtyard—we'll steal a truck or something. Come on. Fuentes is dead, too."

"Esta bien," the girl whispered. She ran toward the head of the stairs. Track broke into a long-strided commando walk along the corridor—the girl was dead weight. The two men Pedro had left guarding the staircase had moved to the first floor and were positioned now behind a barricade of two overstuffed chairs and an overturned table, trading shots with guards who were at the rear of the house. Track sprinted down the stairs, calling to the female prisoner and the two men with her. "We hit the bottom, burn out your rifles toward the enemy position. We'll hit the door and make for the courtyard. Save some ammo for the courtyard. You'll need it."

As they circled down the stairs to the barricaded position Track turned toward the enemy fire, swung his M-16 on line and shouted to the other three, "Open fire—now!"

His ears rang with it, hot brass pelting toward his face and neck, the girl with an M-16 in each hand, firing both of them as though she'd been doing it all her life. The two men with Track reached the base of the stairs and sprinted toward the doorway leading from the house. When they reached the door, they crouched and laid down fire as Track moved closer to the doors, the M-16 firing from his right hand. The girl was shouting something he could not catch. The two men who had taken cover behind the barricade were up, running for the doors, as well, firing toward the guard positions at the rear of the house.

At the door Track dropped the M-16 from his right hand to let it hang on its sling at his side. He shifted the unconscious girl to free up his left hand for the second M-16. He worked off the safety awkwardly with his left thumb, set it to auto, then shoved the weapon forward, tense against its sling, and fired.

The girl and two of the men flanked him into the courtyard. It was a study in confusion; armed men were rushing everywhere, but none of them seeming to care exactly where. Track surveyed the terrain; there was a van parked near the open gates and security vehicles streamed around it into the courtyard. Behind Track, the other two escapees came through the doorway, one of them limping badly, half-supported by the second man.

A man moved into view from the far left side of the van, a lit cigarette in the corner of his mouth. When he saw Track and the prisoners his jaw dropped, the cigarette falling, and he snatched for the .45 in his tanker-style chest rig. Track started to fire, but the girl's twin M-16s fired faster. The man's body slammed back and away from the van. "Get inside," Track ordered. The girl sprinted ahead of him and slid the cargo door open.

In seconds, Track unceremoniously dumped the unconscious Debbie Hinchcliffe on the floor of the van. A security jeep with flashing mars lights raced toward the van, the man in the front passenger seat firing an M-16. Track scored a hit and the assault rifleman's body slumped back, rolling from the jeep along the vehicle's back end.

Both assault rifles empty, with no time to reload, Track's right hand flashed to the X-15 rig and his fist closed around the butt of the P-38. He ripped the pistol from the leather, upping the safety into the fire position as he thrust the weapon toward the driver of the security jeep and fired repeatedly. The man's face seemed to shatter beneath the peak of his OD baseball cap. The jeep careered wildly to Track's right, jumped the low stone barrier that separated the courtyard from the garden, then continued on, plowing across the garden and impacting on the far wall. Nothing happened for an instant. Then the jeep was suddenly engulfed in a fireball—black and orange against the gray dawn sky, belching upward.

Track wrenched open the driver's door of the van and jumped onto the seat, hand groping for the key. "Shit!" There was no key.

Track stretched out across the seat and lowered the top of his body beneath the dashboard, his right hand reaching for the Fazendeiro. The van was old enough; there was no steering wheel lock. He found the right wires, one-handed the Fazendeiro open and cut the wires. He touched the cut ends of the two wires together to generate the spark he needed, twisted them together and revved the engine.

Sometimes, he thought, righting himself in the seat, it was a handy thing to have been raised on the south side of Chicago.

Two more of the escapees had reached the van. Track started to ease the van forward now, cutting the wheel sharply right, then giving the van more gas. He intersected the remaining two excapees' path, shouting to the girl behind him, "Tell your friends to jump on. Hurry!"

The girl shouted in Spanish. Track slowed the van. The injured man was aboard—and then the second man. The shouted from behind him, "Go! Go!"

Track stomped the clutch, upshifted and let the clutch bounce up, hammering down on the gas pedal as he cut the wheel hard left. "Guards at the gates—shoot 'em!"

He could hear gunfire from inside the van, behind him now. The guards at the gates started to fall back as Track stomped the clutch again, upshifting, then giving the van a full shot of gas.

The gates were a blurr on either side, then gone. Ahead a security jeep blazed assault-rifle fire from the passenger seat. Track snatched the P-38 from his trouser band and fired through the open window, emptying the 9 mm at the gunman aboard the jeep. The jeep veered hard right, to Track's left, bouncing the curb up onto the parkway and disappeared from sight.

Track didn't look back. There wasn't time.

13

Maria Sanchez had abandoned the rendezvous point as she had agreed to. Track drove through the countryside toward the secondary rendezvous, hoping she was waiting. The girl bandaged the leg of the wounded escapee. Track had watched her in the mirror. Now she sat on the passenger seat beside him in silence as he rolled the van, headlights off, slowly along the country roads to the east of the city, toward the secondary rendezvous.

The girl finally spoke. "What is your name, *señor*?"

"Dan—Dan Track. And how are you called, *niña*?"

She laughed. "I am not a little girl. I have sixteen years, Dan Track. I am a woman. In the prison there beneath the presidential palace, I have been raped fourteen times. I have fought with the Resistance since I am thirteen, and I have killed many men and women. I am not a little girl."

"Touché," Track said, smiling.

"Touché?"

"French—it means you made your point."

"Ah, *bueno*. Why are you here?"

"What is your name?" Track asked again.

"Lupe."

"You're kidding?" Track laughed.

"What is this kidding?"

"Joking. But 'Lupe'—the name is a stereotype almost."

"What is a—how you call it?" she asked, smiling.

"Never mind. I'm surprised you can smile after all you have done."

She looked at him, then nodded. "You are smiling, Dan Track."

The sky was a deep metallic gray and in the half light he could see her features clearly. "What will you do now that you're free?"

"I am not free. I have the chance to fight against the forces of El General again. And perhaps I shall stay alive. Perhaps I shall die. But I will never be captured again. And I will never be free until the men of El General are all dead."

"But with Fuentes dead," Track began. "Then—"

"The drug smugglers will not surrender their money. They will make more bloodshed. The fighting will continue."

"Has it become a way of life?" Track asked her.

She didn't answer him, but turned her face away to stare out the window.

TRACK STOPPED THE VAN about five hundred yards off the road in a grove of trees. As he stepped out Maria Sanchez came running from the trees and into his arms. "Dan, I was so afraid." She hugged him tightly and Track held her for a moment.

"What about the rest of the escapees?"

"All that I could do was to point them in the right direction, so they could rendezvous with the leaders of the Resistance and pray to the Virgin Mother that they would make it safely. I waited long past the time you were to return. I could hear the gunfire. But once it was too light I..."

"I know." Track nodded, releasing her. "Here, hold my gun a minute." Track stripped off the shoulder rig with the Walther P-38 and handed it to her. The Bianchi X-15 rig was nearly dry. As he walked around the front of the van, he peeled off the sweater, feeling a sudden chill as he freed the still semisodden garment from his body. He stripped off the shirt, as well, throwing it and the sweater on the floor of the van through the open side door.

"Maria, meet Lupe."

"I know Lupe," Maria revealed, smiling, hugging the sixteen-year-old girl. "She is one of us."

"I sort of figured that," Track said, smiling. "And—meet Debbie." Debbie had awakened perhaps an hour before and screamed so loudly while trying to claw or strike every person near her that it had been necessary to have her bound and gagged. "Debbie? Would you like to say hello. We're all friends here." Track reached across and undid the gag that was tied to the nape of her neck. As he moved his hands away, her teeth locked onto his right wrist.

As Track tried to free his wrist, Maria reached past him and slapped the girl hard on the cheek. Track inspected the mark on his wrist. "Did she break skin, Dan?"

"No, but it's not that she didn't try. She probably just hasn't had her teeth sharpened lately."

Maria grabbed Debbie by both shoulders and shook her. "Ungrateful *puta*—why do you do this thing? Answer me!"

"He killed El General!" She screamed the words and then began to sob.

Maria stepped back and turned to Track. "This is true?"

Track licked his lips. "Partly. A guy named Pedro—one of the escapees. I don't remember his last name—"

In unison Maria and Lupe murmured, "Pedro de Santiago Vargas."

"He shot El General, who then shot him. Fuentes was barely alive when I put a burst into his head."

Maria made the sign of the cross over her chest. "Revolution...it has begun. And you, Dan, you will be hunted everywhere. Give up on the girl. You will have a better chance of getting out of the country without her."

"No. I came for her. I leave with her." He looked at Maria. "You said there was an escape route. I need it."

Maria didn't answer for a moment, then somberly nodded. *"Sí—esta bien,"* she told Lupe. "Take the vehicle and the others—you know the place.'' Lupe nodded. ''And you and you—'' she called to the two healthiest looking of the escapees ''—on the other side of the trees, I have a car. Put this one—'' she gestured toward Debbie ''—in the back seat. And gag her again.'' She turned back to Track. ''We must hurry, Dan. I had your luggage stolen from your hotel. There are clean clothes for you.''

''She's gonna need some clothes.'' Track gestured toward Debbie.

''*Sí.* Where we go I will find some.''

The two men were carrying Debbie Hinchcliffe from the van, her body wriggling, her muffled cries of protest sounding almost animallike. As Track started from the van, grabbing his wet shirt, retaking his shoulder rig from Maria, he felt hands on his bare shoulders and back and he turned around. Lupe circled her arms around his neck and she seemed almost to launch herself toward him. His right arm curled around her waist as she kissed him hard on the mouth. ''I like you, Dan Track. My bed—it is yours if you ever wish it.'' She smiled and then ran toward the front of the van, looking off toward the road. Track stared after her a moment and then started after Maria.

14

François Bastogne walked across the courtyard. Medical personnel crouched beside those still alive; uniformed guards, some of them wounded, moved the bodies of the dead.

Chet Halston was nowhere to be found.

To Bastogne it was merely a matter of adding two and two. Halston had sent in someone very good, either from the States or perhaps from the Sicilian Mafia. Whoever the hitman had been, the fellow had had the foresight to free all the prisoners in the cells beneath the presidential palace and utilize them to his advantage.

But that it was a hit on Fuentes was clear. The burst in the head was classic.

Professional.

And the girl was gone.

Halston had made his play. There was no time, Bastogne realized, stopping beside a gutted, smoking jeep, to contact his associates in Marseilles. Halston was trying to take over Fuentes's cocaine trade.

And the people in Marseilles would not want that.

His eyes scanned the courtyard. Colonel Rodriguez had assumed command of the presidential palace, restricting entry of foreign and domestic media, and releasing an official statement that Communist terrorists had performed great acts of violence but that the nation was still secure. He had declared martial law. That, Bastogne had found particularly amusing. Ever since the coup that had enabled Fuentes to seize power there had been nothing but martial law.

Bastogne walked toward Rodriguez, planning what he would say, what he would offer and how he would offer it. It was safe to assume that Rodriguez could control the Communists, yet still appear to be right wing, as Fuentes had done before him. But Rodriguez could not control the American Mafia—not without help.

Bastogne stopped a few paces from Rodriguez and called out, "Hernando, may I speak with you a moment, old friend?"

Rodriguez dismissed the enlisted man he had been speaking to with a gesture of his hand as he turned around. "Yes, François? What is it?"

"I must speak with you," Bastogne began taking his cigarettes from the breast pocket of his long-sleeved white shirt and putting one in his mouth.

"I thought that you might, François."

"You are, how should I say it—" Bastogne smiled "—taking over?"

"Yes."

"You will need money."

"Yes."

"You will need guns."

"Yes," Rodriguez replied, nodding.

"Halston is not the only one with guns and money. Instead of M-16s, I can give you your choice of any assault rifle in the world. Instead of dollars, I can pay you in any currency. I wish to help you. But you must help me. Halston's men—they did this. The assassin who so brutally murdered El General worked for Halston. That is why Halston fled with him. And they have taken the girl. She can be the key to power in this thing."

"You ask that I do what?" Rodriguez murmured.

"Halston's man would not keep the girl here. They would flee the country. They cannot escape by sea. Nor by air. They must travel toward the Mexican border, the mountainous wild country there. There are thousands of places where they might cross. We must intercept them. We must kill the man. We must retake the girl. And if Halston is with them..."

"If—" Rodriguez smiled, his handsome, almost boyish face showing amusement "—we kill a representative of the American Mafia, we shall have them all down on us."

"But no, *mon ami*. My people will support you. You have nothing to fear. If we control the girl, we have intelligence data at our disposal that could cost La Cosa Nostra untold millions of Yankee dollars. We would be immune to their threats. We could have the power."

"I shall order men into the countryside. I shall establish a base near the border. When the girl is found, I must be there."

"*We* must be there," Bastogne corrected. Rodriguez smiled, paused, then, taking a disposable lighter from his fatigues, he lit Bastogne's cigarette.

15

The water pressure was low, the temperature was tepid, but at least it was water and clean, and the soap and shampoo and the towel Maria Sanchez had left for Track made up for its inadequacies. He had washed his body twice, his hair three times, after brushing and flossing his teeth and using a shot glass of Smirnoff 100 as a mouthwash. If he had swallowed any water while going through the tunnel, there would be interesting times ahead, he thought. Interesting, but not pleasant. He had been standing under the water for several minutes, rinsing his body, trying to store energy for the ordeal ahead. That he had had no sleep wasn't going to help much. That Debbie could not be trusted wouldn't help, either. He would not be able to close his eyes on the road.

Track shut off the water, grabbed the towel beyond the shower curtain and started to dry himself. It was a single-story farmhouse a hundred miles or so away from the capital; it had electricity, but the cooking was apparently done on a massive wooden hearth, as it likely had been done in such houses for a century or more.

He began to dress—a fresh pair of Levi's, a light blue snap-front cowboy shirt, and the spare pair of cowboy boots, the uniform of his cover. He would have preferred combat boots, but the cowboy boots were comfortable enough and would have to do. The P-38, which he had cleaned before cleaning himself, he stuffed in the waistband of his Levi's under the carved wide belt with the brass trophy buckle in the shape of a longhorn skull. He had selected the buckle for one reason only—it was solid brass, heavy and the horns of the skull were thick and sharp. It would make an acceptable flail. In the old days of Chicago, the uniform of the day had been the wide, black, Marine Corps style Garrison straps with squared-off brass buckles. You would take the belt and thread it through both ends of the buckle, round and round until the entire interior area was packed with leather. Sixteen or eighteen inches of strap was left loose and held in the fist. The buckle and rolled strap with over a foot of play made a formidable weapon for swatting someone in the head or face or throat.

But that was another world. Or was it?

He walked the narrow corridor toward the rear of the house where he could hear talking.

In the kitchen, Maria at the table, setting out plates, and the woman who owned the farm—Track had already been introduced to her—was cooking by the hearth. The woman's name was Señora Gomez. No other name or names had been offered.

Maria smiled, looking up. "Sit down, Dan. We will get food into you. I told Señora Gomez you are *norteamericano*—she is careful what she cooks." Maria laughed.

Track smiled and took the wooden chair at the end of the table that overlooked both the kitchen door that led outside into the yard and the corridor leading to the front of the house.

"You can put your pistol on the table," Maria told him, putting down more plates of steaming vegetables. "Señora Gomez will not mind." Track was staring at the vegetables. He looked up as Maria began to laugh. "And you can eat the vegetables. Señora Gomez and her husband—he is away in the capital—use chemical fertilizer in their fields, not the kind you were thinking of."

Tracked smirked. "I know, after your stint as a model, you had a mind-reading act, right?"

She sat down at the chair on his left, resting her chin in her cupped right palm, her blue eyes sparkling. "You have a woman. Tell me about her."

It was a statement, not a question.

"What makes you think that?"

"You are not married, but you tried nothing with me at my house. And there is a look in your eyes—of confidence. A great deal of it. So, you must have a woman. A fine woman."

"Her name's Desiree."

"She is French, no? Bastogne is French."

"She's half-French, half-Swiss. Who's Bastogne?"

Maria leaned back in her chair. "They sent you here and did not tell about Bastogne?"

"No."

"You know of Señor Chet Halston."

"The Mafia guy." Track nodded. "Yeah, I know of Señor Chet Halston."

"Bastogne is with the French counterpart—whatever it is called. From Marseilles. I think maybe they are worse than the Mafia. His mother was born here, but she is French. He was raised here but then went back to France—for many years. He came back and he buys cocaine and he works with El General. He is good to his mother, but he is a killer. He is very good-looking."

"Well, I'm glad he's nice to his mother," Track said, smiling. "Should I worry about Bastogne?"

"He is a very greedy man and very ambitious I think. With the death of El General, there could be much trouble because of Bastogne and Halston. But perhaps each will think the other was responsible."

"Let me ask you a question," Track said, looking at his hands for a moment, then taking the pistol from his trouser band and setting it on the table beside him. "You're sure Señora Gomez speaks no English?"

"*Sí.* But she can be trusted."

"I don't doubt that. But you said you were Fuentes's mistress at times—"

"Twice," she interrupted, her smile fading. "For six months once. You wish to understand the North American girl, no?"

"Yes."

"You are not a woman, so you cannot. But I will try to explain. There are some women who enjoy being brutalized or beaten. Perhaps—perhaps they feel guilt because of sex, perhaps the beating itself sexually stimulates them. I do not know. I was never one of these—" her eyes brightened for an instant "—and I can see you are not such a man who would do this to a woman. But Ignacio—El General—he was such a man. He did not use strange objects, but his hands would slap at a woman, his feet kick her. His belt—often his belt." Maria lowered her eyes. "Very often, his belt. He, ah, he was a very cruel lover, yet a very accomplished lover. Once—once even I begged him to come to me again. I could not help myself. It was as though Satan were upon you and somehow it was good. You cannot understand." Maria made the sign of the cross. "But Debbie—she has never known someone such as Fuentes. Perhaps there is no one else such as him—praise be to God this is true. But her mind—I think her mind is changed—to something strange. She wanted what he gave her. He is dead. Perhaps she has made love to many other men and never did she experience such a thing. She hates you because you have taken her greatest pleasure from her. She will kill you for it, I think. If you let her."

"How did you, ah..."

"Survive El General?"

"Yes," Track whispered.

"By hating him. But what it did to me inside, I did not survive that, I think. Ignacio—he could not touch without hurting, without pain." Maria pushed her chair back from the table, stood up, and, wrapping herself slowly in her shawl, walked away toward the kitchen door. She stood there—not turning around, not speaking—for a very long time.

16

"So, you're Rudy."

"Yes, sir."

"I understand that you were very faithful to Don Carlo."

"The don, sir, the don was like a second father to me, like a grandfather to my..."

"Yes, that is very good. Loyalty is a fine thing. I have a job for you. I understand that before the untimely death of Don Carlo he had put you on light duty due to some injuries you received in Mexico."

"Yes, sir."

"And that now you are well you are no longer interested in merely guarding the whorehouse."

"Yes, sir."

"That's fine. I'm sending you and four other boys down past Mexico. You'll be in charge of the other boys, and you'll take you orders directly from Mr. Halston."

"Yes, sir."

"Rudy, Mr. Halston is one of our most important people concerning the drug operation."

"The don, sir, he..."

"The don was part of the past. He could afford to keep his hands clean of drugs. But the don—God rest his soul—is gone. If you wish to continue in the business, then you must be prepared to be involved with drugs."

Rudy squirmed in his chair. His father had avoided drugs. Don Carlo had avoided drugs. The don had forbidden any of his family to be involved in the dirty business. But it was no longer a family, Rudy realized. But there was his own family. His wife. His children. With no formal education and only one employer since he was fourteen and that employer not one he could give as a reference, Rudy's options were limited. "Yes, sir. When do I leave?"

"This afternoon, Rudy. Now, about the man who is your target. Mr. Halston was involved in a disagreement with a rival firm—from Marseilles. You know where that is, Rudy?"

"Yes, sir." He had read books; Marseilles was in France. And he had locked horns with the Marseilles underworld people once. They were tough and liked knives as much as his own people liked guns.

"The Marseilles people are led by a man known as Bastogne—locally, that is, and that's all you need to concern yourself with...the local picture. Apparently the former leader of the country was assassinated by someone from the Marseilles organization at Bastogne's request. This person has taken with him—by force, Mr. Halston has learned—a certain young lady. She is very important to us. You'll help Mr. Halston to recover the young woman, see to it the man from Marseilles dies and escort the young lady to a destination Mr. Halston will disclose. Then you'll report back to me. You'll be dropped in Mexico right at the border. You'll learn your final destination when you arrive. You can bring personal weapons and any other useful equipment since there won't be any border crossings to worry about. But no ID or anything."

"Right, sir."

"Goodbye Rudy. And, of course, good luck."

Rudy stared at the man across the desk. The man had not looked directly at him once. Nor would he now.

Dismissed, Rudy got up and left the office.

TRACK HAD SLEPT for six hours. Maria had roused him at 7:00 P.M. local time. He pulled on his clothes and the X-15 rig and resettled the P-38 in the leather. He followed her along the corridor, then through the kitchen door and into the night.

Track heard the horses before saw them.

Maria spoke. "We shall travel—"

"We?"

"You cannot watch the girl as another woman can watch her and you cannot trust her. I shall go with you. I have two other men. Both are named Juan. One is tall and the other is short and a little fat, it will not be confusing to you. We shall travel by horseback. It is the only way."

He pulled the cowboy hat over his eyes as he stopped at the middle of the yard. Five horses. He knew very little about horses. "We shall travel until after midnight. There will be a safe place where we can rest. And then a long day's journey to the border with Mexico."

Track approached a powerful gray, stroking its forehead.

"You may ride this one if you wish," Maria said, patting the animal's neck. "Juan—the tall one—told me the animal's name. He is El Cuchillo. It means..."

"I know what it means," Track almost whispered. "The knife." Track smiled. The horse went nicely with the cowboy boots and the hat. He was definitely going to punch out that DEA man.

BASTOGNE STRAPPED ON his gun belt as he walked. The command helicopter, a Bell Long Ranger, had landed in the courtyard of the presidential palace and Colonel Hernando Rodriguez was standing some short distance away from it, surrounded by his officers.

Bastogne settled the belt just below his waist, drawing the ivory-gripped Browning GP from the hand-carved open-top holster. He drew the slide back, letting it run forward, chambering the top round from the magazine. He locked the thumb safety into the "up" position, then reholstered the 9 mm. He stopped walking as he closed the safety strap across the grip just beneath the tang.

Rodriguez was being marvelously cooperative. But once Rodriguez had the girl in his possession, the story might well change.

Bastogne mentally weighed the odds. Then began walking again. The knot of officers surrounding Rodriguez opened for him.

"Hernando, *mon ami,*" Bastogne began...

MEXICO WAS A DECENT COUNTRY, as primitive countries went, Chet Halston thought absently, sitting on the veranda of the family-owned villa, watching the sun sink. You could do okay with the local officials. They'd leave you alone as long as you left them alone. And that was pretty good in itself.

He sipped at his whiskey. Tomorrow he'd hop in the car and the driver would take him to the airfield. There Halston would greet the boys and give them the final details of what they were supposed to do.

This guy from the Marseilles underworld—he'd be as hot as a two-dollar pistol, Halston thought. And getting across the border would be the only way to go. Into Mexico. Wherever he crossed the border, he'd need a telephone quick—to order up air transport, to report in—for a whole bunch of reasons, as Halston saw it. The border area itself was small, but big enough that a sharp guy might get past anybody looking for him. But the nearest telephone was in a town called Los Quatros Santos. Which "four saints" he didn't know, but the sinners were familiar.

He wanted the man dead.

He wanted the girl alive.

Chet Halston slipped again at his whiskey and watched the reddish coppery disk of sun float downward. He raised his glass and murmured, "Here's to you, El General. Rest in pieces," he toasted, and then laughed.

17

Track nudged his knees gently against the big gray, the horse rocking under him as it mounted, crossed and descended a grassy hillock along the otherwise gentle slope leading through the fringe of the jungle into the mountains. The sun was nearly gone. Behind him, Debbie, her wrists bound in front of her to the horn of her saddle, one ankle tied into the stirrup, was being led by the reins by one of the Juans—the tall thin one—who rode just ahead of her. Riding drag was Juan number two, the short fat one.

Track looked forward. Maria had been riding ahead, but now she was reining in the big black. Track nudged his animal ahead, to a position beside Maria. Her horse reared slightly; she cooed to it and it fell into an even gait as Track and Maria rode side by side.

"The *norteamericana*—she has not spoken."

"We're probably lucky." Track quipped, smiling. "I'm sure she'll have something to say at the right moment."

"I have instructed the two Juans that she be gagged if it becomes necessary."

Track nodded.

Maria spoke again. "Tell me about this woman you call Desiree?"

"She's very pretty. She has eyes like yours. I've been in love with her for a long time. One of these days we plan to get married."

"And where is she now?"

"In Switzerland with a man named Zulu who is her confidant and bodyguard, and her friend. My friend, too, I guess."

"Do you have any other family?"

"Compiling an obituary just in case?" Track joked, laughing.

"A man is not alone, nor does he just have a woman. Friends?"

"Okay. I have a nephew named George. He's getting married soon. George's father, my brother-in-law, is a nice guy. Got a good friend named Sir Abner Chesterton. I used to work for him. Maybe I still do. Sometimes I'm not so sure. A Russian couple, Sergei and Tatiana, they're good friends, too. Got a secretary named Tassles LaToure who I don't see very often. She's in her sixties. Got a cat named Dorothy. Don't see her very often, either. Some other people I know—that's about it. Now, how about you?"

Track looked at her as he guillotined the tip from a cigar and began patting himself down for his Zippo.

"I am alone. Ever since...I am alone."

"No lover?" he asked, realizing as he asked that it was too direct a question. He thought about how to change the subject as he lit his cigar, but she had already begun to answer.

"I had a lover. When I began to see El General—because of what I had to do—he, ah, he took his own life."

"I'm sorry."

Track took the opportunity to survey the terrain. The vegetation on their left was dense, the edge of the jungle itself. On their right, as though some magic boundary line had been crossed, it was very sparse. The sun was gone now, only a wash of purple remaining as a reminder of the day.

Maria finally broke the silence. "I am sorry, too. I wish you very good fortune with your love, Dan—with this woman with the beautiful name. Do not spend too much time away from her. Do not spend too much time doing other things. If you die without being married, she will grieve for you even more, I think." Maria looked away.

"Are you entering Mexico with me?" Track asked her suddenly.

"I must return to my country. With El General gone, the fighting will be more serious now. Everyone will be needed."

"I wish, well, that I could have done more," Track told her.

"If the North American girl is this important and you are able to get her away, you will have done a great deal. But you must promise me that if you cannot, if something should go wrong, then—then you must..."

"Kill her." Track finished it. It wasn't a promise, it was a statement of the obvious. Track knew that the obvious was sometimes the hardest thing to see.

18

The girl had told them to keep her bound or she would attempt to escape. They had kept her bound. But Track did not like it, primarily because he realized that somehow, in some way he didn't even want to consider, Debbie did like it. She would not walk to her horse at dawn when they had saddled up and prepared to begin the all-day, all-night ride that he hoped would get them into Mexico. She had forced them to carry her. She had refused to mount her animal. Track had lifted her and thrown her into the saddle, tying her again to the saddle horn as Maria knotted the cord round her right ankle to the stirrup. Track had not liked the look in the girl's cycs. Whcn hc handlcd hcr roughly, thcrc was a distant glimmer of sexual desire. He had turned away, swung onto his own mount, then started up the trail ahead of Maria and the others.

The Rolex read 9:30 A.M. as Track took his canteen from the saddle horn and drank. Maria was beside him again.

Maria spoke. "This girl—she worries me. Last night I slept near her. She was...she was..."

"Delerious. I heard it." Track screwed the cap back onto the canteen and wound the strap a few times around the horn so if he was forced to put the animal to a gallop he wouldn't lose his water supply.

"I think she is crazy."

"What happened with El General. It may have been more traumatic an experience for her than either of us suspects," Track told Maria, not sure he believed his own words.

"How did the daughter of a United States senator get to be this way?"

Track shrugged. "They didn't tell me the story of her life. What I gather is that after her mother died her father took her with him everywhere. He was an ambassador in the Middle East, in South America—like that. She was in and out of schools all over the place. She got kicked out of a bunch of eastern universities and he sent her west. She was paying another girl to take her place in class to keep her father cooled down. She just seemed to have this passion for getting into trouble. Used the name Debbie Davis."

"What if she did not just use a name? What if Debbie Davis is a separate person?"

Track looked at Maria. "I know, when you weren't a model or a mind reader, you were a shrink. Right?"

"I have read a great deal about the workings of the human mind."

"Listen, Maria, I'm just the guy they tapped to get her out of here, not figure her out. I mean, it would be helpful but there isn't time."

"*Sí*. But it is interesting—frightening to consider. Perhaps she has an alter ego that wishes to be abused, wishes to be dominated. It's not impossible with a little girl who has no mother and a very busy father."

"And who are you, Freud or Adler?" Track asked, smiling.

"I wish that I were either of them, then perhaps I could help this girl." Maria seemed lost in thought.

"Then let me ask you a question, Señorita Doctor. If push comes to shove and she and I wind up in a situation where she'll be taken alive unless I kill her, who would I be killing? Debbie Hinchcliffe or Debbie Davis? Because both of them would wind up dead, wouldn't they?"

Maria fell silent for a long minute, then opened her mouth as if beginning to answer. It was then that Track heard the sound along the trail behind them. He looked up and back.

A helicopter, then another and then a third. Under his breath he snarled, "How do you say 'aw shit' in Spanish, Maria?" But he didn't wait for her reply. He shouted to the two Juans. "Helicopters! *Soladados! Andele amigos!*"

Track thwacked Maria's horse on the rump, then glanced behind him once more, undoing the M-16 quickly from the saddle thongs and using the muzzle like a quirt against his gray's backside. "Gyaagh!" Digging in his heels, Track spurred the gray ahead along the trail, shouting to Maria, "Will it do any good to get into the jungle?"

"Not here!"

Track slowed his mount and waited for the two Juans and Debbie, letting all three riders pass him. He looked skyward again—the helicopters were closing in. There was no doubt the helicopters had spotted them. Track decided on an experiment. Settling the gray with his knees, the reins in his teeth, he lifted the M-16 to his shoulder.

His right thumb found the selector and he located the bubble of the center chopper, the nearest one, in his sights.

He fired. The distance was under two hundred yards. The horse lurched once under him but did not run. His thumb found the selector again, moving it into the auto mode. He squeezed the trigger tight, sending eight rounds toward the advancing center chopper.

There was no gunfire in response.

Track set the selector back to safe, then took the reins from his teeth and wrenched at them, bringing the gray's head around, then digging in his heels.

They wouldn't shoot. They wanted the girl alive.

The gray charged ahead along the path, narrowing the distance between Track and the other riders. The assault rifle in his right fist, the reins bunched in his left, Track flattened himself out against the animal beneath him, the gray's mane lashing at his face in the slipstream, sweat and froth spraying him.

The noise of the helicopter rotors was louder now behind and above them. Track shouted to Maria,

"Keep close to Debbie. Keep close and they can't shoot!"

As Track cut down the distance separating them he could see that Debbie's face was turned upward, almost expectantly.

Track wondered what she wanted. One of the helicopters was almost directly overhead now, hovering, then leapfrogging forward, then hovering again, its shadow drawing out along the trail behind them.

Through a loudspeaker system from one of the choppers—Track thought it was the one directly over their head—a voice blared in heavily accented English, "This is Colonel Hernando Rodriguez, successor to El General Ignacio Fuentes. You are ordered to stop your animals, to throw down your weapons, to raise your hands over your heads!"

Track knew no one aboard the helicopter could hear him, but he shouted anyway, "Fuck you!" He stabbed the M-16 skyward and he fired into the underbelly of the chopper. The chopper pilot seemed to lose it for a minute, taking off at a right angle to the trail and downward, almost to the level of the trail, then pulling it up rapidly over the treetops.

The voice on the loudspeaker was less confident now, almost afraid. "Throw down your weapons or you will be fired upon!"

Track thwacked the barrel of the M-16 against his horse's rump again. He passed the fat Juan and came parallel with the horse that Debbie rode, was tied to. Track put the reins for his own animal into his teeth and grabbing at the girl's reins, shouting to the skinny Juan, "Let her go! *Ahora!*"

With both sets of reins in his left fist, he pointed the M-16 at the girl's head.

Track looked skyward and waited.

The three helicopters hovered in position. The girl's horse was becoming skittish. Maria rode up to sooth it.

Debbie's eyes were wide and alert—but not with fear.

The voice came over the loudspeaker again. "You would not shoot her. She is the daughter of one of your *norteamericano* senators!"

Track arced the M-16 rifle to his left and fired three rounds into the brush, then brought it back on target.

"All right. You win this round, *señor.* But we shall return."

The lead chopper started almost straight upward, banked steeply to port, spinning 180 degrees on its vertical axis, then headed west, followed by the other two.

Debbie finally spoke. "Would you have shot me?"

"No," Track whispered. "Not this time."

19

The sun was hot and very nearly directly overhead. Bastogne took the straw panama from his head, wiping his brow with a silk handkerchief, then wiping the inside of the hat, as well. The sweatband was sodden to the touch. Beside where he stood, Rodriguez squatted on the ground. The wind blew hard, in long, almost endless-seeming gasps across the flat top of the mesa where the three helicopters had landed. The man on the ground who had fired the assault rifle at them had hit the fuselage three times, and Bastogne's heart had leaped to his mouth. But there had been no serious damage.

Bastogne pondered what should be the next course of action.

"We can kill the *norteamericana*," Rodriguez suggested.

"And what will all of this have been for then, *mon ami*?"

Rodriguez looked up at Bastogne through the cigar smoke ballooning around Rodriguez's face. "And what would you suggest? If I put troops down they might not stop him before he crosses the border into Mexico. If I pursue with helicopters, he might kill her. What would you suggest?"

"The fact that he takes her to Mexico means that he wants her alive. He might kill her on this side of the border, but he would never kill her once he has crossed it. I have given this considerable thought, Hernando. He will need to contact Halston and the Cosa Nostra people. They could not possibly have a rendezvous set. There are too many variables. What if the border were to be sealed for days or weeks? What if a thousand things had happened and he had to take her across the border in some other manner. They may have a floating rendezvous—where a plane or a car comes to a certain place at a certain time each night. Or, perhaps some other arrangement. But not something concrete waiting for him."

"I do not understand you," Rodriguez said loudly over the keening of the wind. "I do not understand you at all, François."

"Deborah Hinchcliffe is very important to us all. Once this Mafia assassin has her across the border, we cannot be used as scapegoats. So he will not kill her. If we can corner him, we can offer him a bribe to get her away from him. Then we kill him. Or can we attack in force and kill him. He will not have time to kill the girl."

"Perhaps."

Bastogne laughed. "It is well to remember, Hernando, that dead this girl is worth nothing to us. Or to our *amigo* Chet Halston. Dead, the score is even. But if we have her alive..."

"Then we have power," Rodriguez completed, nodding. "But I cannot invade Mexico; it would be most awkward."

"Your soldiers can remove the identifying patches from their uniforms."

"No. There is a better way. Come with me." Rodriguez got up from the ground in one fluid motion, as though rising from a chair. Bastogne fell into step with him and they headed toward the command helicopter. "The terrorists can do anything and not jeopardize their position. Whatever they do, they are still only terrorists. They will stop this Mafia killer and get us the girl."

"And why shouldn't they just take the girl for themselves?" Bastogne argued.

"Because we shall take the terrorist camp and hold their leader. Come!" Rodriguez broke into a run signaling his chopper pilot to start the rotors.

THERE WAS NOWHERE TO RUN, so they walked the horses at a comfortable pace along the trail paralleling the jungle fringe. Debbie had begun gouging her nails into her wrists to draw blood and it had been necessary to glove her hands and rebind them in such a way that she could neither pull of the gloves nor abrade her wrists with the ropes.

There was no time to rest, but the animals were tired. Track signaled for a dismount. "Let's lead the animals for a while." He started ahead; Maria caught up with him.

"What's bugging you?" Track asked Maria.

"You are not going to kill the girl if it is needed."

"No, I'm not."

"Then, if Rodriguez has replaced El General, he shall have her."

"No, he won't," Track told her flatly, tugging harder at the reins, drawing the gray ahead. The M-16 was strapped across his back now, muzzle down. If the helicopters returned now, there would be no time to set up a counterassault.

Maria had told him there were six or seven hours of hard riding to the border.

How many miles that was, Track did not know. He had not checked the map since morning.

This successor to El General, this successor to the guns-cocaine-money business. This Rodriguez would try something again.

Of that Track was certain.

He looked back down the trail at Debbie. What he saw in her pretty eyes looked more and more like madness.

CHET HALSTON WAITED inside the air-conditioned limousine. He had always prided himself on being able to tough it out with the boys as well or better than any of them. He had proven that again. Shooting his way out of the presidential palace courtyard, stealing that jeep to make it to the city limits, hot-wiring that second car and driving all night to get across the border—not bad, he thought.

So he was entitled to a rest, he told himself. He could wait in the limo.

The leader of the team from Florida, the nearest family organization he could trust, was a young punk named Rudy. He didn't know anything else about him, but he could tell the skinny guy walking from the Beechcraft that had just landed had to be Rudy. The guy quickened his pace, running toward the limousine now. He wasn't visibly armed—but that didn't matter.

You could always tell a lot about a guy, Halston thought, by his choice of personal weapons. It was one reason Halston had structured the thing so they guys wouldn't have to go through customs.

The skinny guy stopped beside the limousine, and Halston threw open the door.

He extended his right hand into the blast furnace of sunlight. "Rudy?"

"Yes, sir. Mr. Halston?"

"Yes. Come on in out of the fuckin' heat, Rudy."

"Thank you, sir." Rudy sat on one of the turned-down rear-facing seats beside the fold-out bar.

"Make yourself a drink, Rudy."

"No thanks, sir. I don't drink when I'm working."

"Make an exception. Have a cold beer. Not the Mexican stuff—American."

"All right, sir." As Rudy turned his attention to the bar, Halston watched him. He had thought originally that Rudy's hair had been blown by the props but now he realized that Rudy was one of those guys who couldn't make his hair stay down no matter what. It gave him the appearance of being rumpled, used.

"Gimme a beer, too. Light. I'm watchin' my calories." Halston laughed.

Rudy uncapped a Michelob Light and passed it over. Then he took a sip of his regular beer. "Very good, sir. Thank you."

"Don't mention it. How much they tell ya?"

"Not much, Mr. Halston," Rudy said, smiling deferentially. "Some gunsel outa Marseille is all—put the snatch on some American girl."

"That's pretty much it, but he's no gunsel. Gotta be real good. Probably one of the top independent assassins—maybe Heinrich or Aquelino or one of them—too good for the Marseilles guys to keep in their stable."

"Yes, sir. We'll watch out for him."

"You'll do more than that, Rudy. I want the guy fuckin' dead—period."

"Certainly, Mr. Halston."

"What kinda gun you carry, Rudy?"

Rudy seemed to hesitate, then smiled. "It's a real old piece, Mr. Halston. My old man gave it to me a long time ago."

"And you still got it. Hey, that's all right. Lemme see."

Rudy licked his lips, then shrugged and reached under his jacket. The pistol was one Halston recognized from the movies. "Lemme see close I won't touch nothin'." Rudy handed him the pistol. "Mauser, right?"

"Yes, sir. A Bolo Mauser, made about 1926."

"What's the caliber?"

"7.63 mm Mauser. Sometimes pretty hard to find."

"How's she load? Down here?" Halston pointed to what should have been the magazine but didn't look right, despite being in front of the trigger guard.

"No, sir. From the top—with stripper clips."

"Hey, that's all right. How many she shoot?"

"Ten rounds in the stripper clip, Mr. Halston."

Halston smiled, weighing the gun in his hand. "She's cute." He handed it back to Rudy. "What else you got?" He made his voice drop, made the words deliberate.

"Each of the boys has his own handgun. We got M-16s, Uzis, shotguns—"

"What kind?" Halston interrupted. "What kinda shotguns?" He read all the magazines and tried to stay current.

"This guy I met a while back—he liked the SPAS 12 by Franci. The guy was a cop, but he used a gun real good. The SPAS impressed me. We're tryin' 'em. So far so good."

"That's the Italian deal, right? Works pump or semiauto."

"Yes, sir. You really seem to know your stuff, Mr. Halston."

"Hey, I was doin' like you guys not too long back. You play it right, Rudy, on this one—next time around maybe you'll be sittin' in the limo givin' the orders."

"Thank you very much, Mr. Halston, but I got no plans to be anythin' but what I am. I'm happy. Got a good family—I mean wife and kids. And the family I work with, well, ever since Don Carlo died—" Rudy crossed himself "—well, things been different. But things been good."

"You suit yourself, Rudy. I got some other guys—locals. They can pull a trigger but they can't think. Gives you a good group. I'll be with ya, too. That cockamamie chauffeur outside—him, too."

"Yes, sir. Where and when?"

"Town called Los Quatros Santos—"

"The four saints, huh?"

"Yeah—like Italian. You're Italian, I can tell. Time was when everybody hadda be Italian. Good for guys like me it changed."

Rudy didn't say anything.

"Anyway, this town Los Quatros Santos—and probably some time late tonight or before noon tomorrow. This guy's gotta be comin' out through the mountains and draggin' this dame with him. He'll go to the phone in the village. We kill him there. All the extra manpower's just insurance."

"What if he makes it to the phone?"

"See my chauffeur? Not too smart. Not too good with a gun—hell, I can outshoot him without even tryin'. But he climbs telephone poles real good." Halston grinned.

Rudy nodded and sipped his beer

20

Without warning it had begun to rain heavily. Maria had planned for most contingencies. Each of the bedrolls was wrapped with a GI-surplus poncho. Track and the others wore theirs now, the ponchos draped to cover the saddles, the bedrolls and as much of themselves as possible.

They had placed a poncho over Debbie when the downpour had begun. She had screamed and shrieked that her body needed the rain. Track told her quietly, "Your body doesn't need the pneumonia," and he had tied the hood of the poncho under her chin so she couldn't attempt to shrug out of it. In the process he and the skinny Juan had gotten themselves soaked.

The animals seemed to step more quickly now, as if the horses as well as the humans who rode them somehow hoped climbing higher into the mountains would take them from the rain. It was a vain hope.

If Rodriguez were to attack, it wouldn't be by helicopter. Not even a lunatic would have stayed airborne in this weather, Track thought. He glanced at his Rolex, a rivulet of water cascading off the poncho as he moved his arm.

Four hours, perhaps five, until the border.

There was a town there, and there was a telephone in the town, and there was a telephone number Track had memorized. He would call and a helicopter would come and take him out and take the girl off his hands.

He wanted that very much. Debbie was self-destructive, masochistic, irrational. "Nuts," he said aloud.

Riding beside him, Maria asked, "What is it you said?"

"Nuts—Debbie Hinchcliffe—she's nuts."

"Sí. Loco."

Track just nodded, more rain running down from the hood as he did, across his face and into his mouth. The poncho smelled of a mixture of talcum powder and rubber and was more than slightly nauseating.

He thought he had given up doing pointless, dumb things when he had left the Army. Obviously not.

BASTOGNE STOOD IN THE RAIN beside Rodriguez as Rodriguez carried on a last-minute strategy session with two captains and a first lieutenant. The first lieutenant asked, "Cololnel, should the third element open fire immediately?"

"No. Wait until they move toward you."

"*Sí*, Colonel."

Rodriguez returned the salutes and slogged back through the mud toward his helicopter, Bastogne struggling to keep up with him. Bastogne asked Rodriguez, "Are you sure this will all go well?"

"Miguel de Cristo is a confidant man. It will never cross his evil mind that I would attempt to take him prisoner. And when it does, it will be too late. And then de Cristo's men will do exactly as they are told and we shall have the girl and the assassin will be dead. And then I will kill de Cristo and appoint my own man to lead the Communistas. With the drug traffic under my control, I will have all the power. Perhaps I will make myself El General—huh?"

Bastogne feigned a smile. Rodriguez was beginning to worry him. "But you will not forget those who had aided you, *mon ami*, eh?"

Rodriguez stopped, stared at him hard. "I will not forget them. If they do not forget themselves. This is my country—and mine alone, François. Come." Rodriguez marched on toward his jeep.

THEY HAD DRIVEN about two miles, at the center of a column of some two-dozen vehicles: jeeps like the one in which they rode and trucks of various weight ranges. The road in some places almost nonexistent as they moved more deeply into the jungle and simultaneously higher into the mountain; miraculously none of the vehicles had as yet become bogged down in the mud. Rodriguez, sitting in the back seat, had been writing something in a small notebook since they had entered the jeep, and Bastogne could no longer contain his curiosity. He turned in his seat beside the driver, looking back directly now. The sounds of the windshield wipers, which were hopelessly inadequate to the task of keeping the rain and splattering mud off the windshield, had become like the throbbing of an aching head to him. He needed conversation and the driver, if not a mute, seemed perfectly capable of imitating one. Bastogne said finally, "Mon Colonel, what is it that you labor so long with? A speech, perhaps?"

Rodriguez looked up, his hair still wet from the rain, a smile in his black eyes. "A speech of sorts, François. It is the eulogy I will delivery for El General."

"Oh."

And Rodriguez laughed. "When you die perhaps I shall make the eulogy for you, *mon ami*."

As Bastogne was trying to think of something to say the radio crackled and the driver, not a mute after all, began speaking into it. There was an exchange of pro-words and then the driver said, "Colonel."

Rodriguez took the microphone. "This is Rodriguez—*diga*."

Bastogne could follow the conversation easily. It was the first lieutenant who had spoken at the conference in the rain. "My men are in position, Colonel; there is no movement from the enemy camp."

"Stay where you are. Be ready. Rodriguez out." Rodriguez spoke again into the microphone. "This is Rodriguez. Elements, Alpha, Bravo—come in."

Another voice—one of the captains. Bastogne didn't remember which. "Alpha Leader. About to break off. Over."

"Rodriguez out. Bravo, come in."

"Bravo element in position, Colonel."

"Rodriguez, out." He handed the microphone back to the driver. As Rodriguez picked up his water-stained baseball cap, he said, "Soon we shall know if the plan works. The attack will begin when I give the word." The driver turned off to the side of the road; one truck peeled away from the column, as well, troops springing from the truck bed to the mud and running forward to guard the jeep. Rodriguez put away his little leather notebook with the eulogy in it. Closing the button on the fatigue blouse flap. "Don't you feel there is something important in this, François? Destiny, perhaps?"

"Yes." Bastogne nodded—evil destiny.

There was an economy and fluidity of movement to Rodriguez Bastogne had not noticed until now. Rodriguez seemed to exit the jeep and don his rain poncho in one almost graceful motion.

Bastogne followed, Rodriguez already holding the receiver of a wireless field telephone.

"This is Rodriguez. Attack! Now!"

As Bastogne struggled into his rain gear he looked at Rodriguez. He seemed flushed with excitement, a child about to embark on an adventure. "Come, François," he said, and set out, his men surrounding him, Bastogne trailing them away from the road and into the jungle. If anything the rain seemed heavier now. The cries of the jungle birds were muted by the pounding rain, and the gunfire crackling in the distance itself sounded odd, like a movie soundtrack.

But Bastogne knew it was real. His older brother had been in the foreign legion and had fought in Vietnam before the Americans had taken over the useless struggle. Bastogne himself had been unwillingly involved in a revolution once. His taste of combat and his brother's recollections of it were more than enough. He was a reluctant player in Rodriguez's game.

Bastogne fished under his poncho for the Browning GP. The holster leather was already sodden to the touch as were his clothes, his boots, his trousers, his hair. His shirt, moderately free of rainwater, was soaked with sweat. It was not just the jungle heat; he was sweating out of fear, too, he knew. Miguel de Cristo was not an easy man to fight against.

More gunfire—some shouting, audible but not intelligible. Rodriguez seemed drawn to the sound of the guns.

Bastogne kept his thumb poised over the 9 mm pistol's safety.

Rodriguez reached under his poncho for his .45 automatic. He raised the pistol high, worked back the slide with his left hand, then broke into a jogging sort of run through the jungle undergrowth.

"Merde," Bastogne moaned, picking up his pace to keep from being left behind.

Rodriguez ran at the head of his men, shouting something that sounded like a prayer to some private god.

There was a burst of automatic weapons' fire; Bastogne threw himself to the ground as the leaves around him seemed to shred under it. One of Rodriguez's men went down.

A booming sound—heavier than the assault-rifle fire. It would be Rodriguez with his .45.

Bastogne was on his knees. Terrorists to the left, firing; Rodriguez firing as he ran toward them.

Bastogne got to his feet and ran in the wake of Rodriguez and his men; there was no choice.

One of de Cristo's men sprang up from a clump of heavy foliage, an M-16 on full-auto spraying toward Rodriguez and his men. Bastogne wheeled to face the sound. He pointed the Browning GP toward the rifleman and emptied the weapon—all thirteen shots—into the man's upper body.

He could hear Rodriguez laughing, shouting, "Bravo! Ha!" Bastogne felt his pants go wet—not from the rain. But he ran on, after Rodriguez and the rest of the men, reloading the Browning with his one spare magazine as he ran.

They left the foliage that grew close to the ground now and were into the trees; there was sporadic assault-rifle fire all around them. As Bastogne worked down the slide stop of the Browning, Rodriguez stopped his headlong dash for the enemy.

Rodriguez was issuing commands into his field telephone. Bastogne steadied his pistol in both hands. He was shaking. He jumped, swinging the pistol around, but it was only Rodriguez. "They tell me—my commanders—that de Cristo is running into the trap under Lieutenant Martinez. So—you are brave, amigo. I shall give you a medal. The first medal I shall award. You will be very proud." As he clapped Bastogne on the back, he laughed, adding, "Or at least you will make it appear so, no?" And then Rodriguez was off again, Bastogne falling in with the rest of the men and running after him.

21

Bastogne was beginning to feel rather heroic. He had saved Hernando Rodrigues from death—in a way at least. And his pants were so wet from the rain that no one would ever notice the testament to his terror. He moved about the muddy rutted square of the tent-and-lean-to village with a certain swagger now, his pistol still in his hand but the safety upped. He thought that if the sun had been shining he would have cast a tall shadow.

Rodriguez's shadow would have dwarfed them all this afternoon. He had taken the headquarters camp of the Communist terrorist leader and de Cristo himself.

De Cristo was handcuffed to two jeeps that had been backed close together, one wrist shackled to each rear bumper.

As Rodriguez approached de Cristo, the rain-soaked and mud-splattered guerrilla leader spat contemptuously. *"¡Hijo de perro!"*

Rodriguez laughed. "You should not speak so disrespectfully, Miguel. I have come here to get your help and cooperation in a matter of grave concern to us both. And you speak so. You should be ashamed." Rodrigues stopped a few inches from de Cristo.

"I would help you with nothing!"

Rodriguez nodded, as though suddenly saddened.

He snapped his fingers and the drivers of the two jeeps started their engines. There was a flash of understanding in de Cristo's eyes. Rodrigues spoke again. "Are you sure you would not care to reconsider, my old friend?"

"Go to hell," he answered in English.

Rodriguez shrugged. "Not very inspired, amigo. Perhaps you need your grasp of the situation broadened." Rodriguez grinned and snapped his fingers again.

The jeeps started to pull away in opposite directions.

Bastogne fought the urge to close his eyes.

De Cristo stood now to his full height, his arms outstretched to what seemed maximum extension, his fingers splayed wide. The jeeps had stopped; apparently Rodriguez had worked it out in advance with his drivers.

Then Rodriguez spoke, confirming Bastogne's suspicion. "The next time, Miguel, that I snap my fingers like this..." he threatened and raised his right hand, his thumb and second finger together. The engines of the jeeps revved loudly, then died to a steady rumble. "The next time, neither vehicle will stop until it reaches the end of the square. And you, well, I know you are very strong, Miguel, but they will rip your arms from the sockets, I think, and the pain will kill you before the bleeding does."

De Cristo licked his lips. The rain still poured down; rivulets of water from his plastered-down hair poured into de Cristo's eyes. They seemed filmed over with hate.

"What will it be? Is there to be a new leader of your guerrillas?"

De Cristo said nothing.

Rodriguez raised his right hand. Bastogne felt bile rising into his throat, burning there as he forced himself to swallow it.

And then de Cristo shouted, "All right!"

Rodriguez walked a little closer to him. "*¡Bueno, amigo—bueno!* I shall tell you what I want your people to do and then you will have your people do it. And if they do it right, you get to keep both arms."

"I will kill you," de Cristo swore.

"Ah, another day, perhaps. Let us worry about this day first, eh?"

Rodriguez snapped his fingers. Bastogne felt his gorge rise again. But the engines of the two jeeps merely stopped.

Rodriguez began to talk to de Cristo as the handcuffs were being removed. "There is a man—a killer who works for the *norteamericanos* in their Mafia thing. He has kidnapped this lovely young lady…." Bastogne would find a quiet place, then he would throw up in private.

THE GIRL HAD BEEN SCREAMING now for some ten minutes. Track liked her better when she was quiet. She had revived some obscenities Track hadn't heard since his boyhood on the south side of Chicago and had even turned a few phrases Track had never heard before at all. She was either very inventive or had made some sort of study of scatology.

He didn't want to know. He just wanted her to stop.

Track reined in his mount. "Whoa, easy boy, steady big fellow." He'd always wanted to say that. He dismounted, his high-heeled cowboy boots sinking into the mud. Track edged past the other riders, using saddles, manes and tails as a lifeline through the treacherous mud.

And then he was beside the girl. She was screaming; this time it was some reference to his relationship with his mother.

Track reached to her right stirrup, flicking the Fazendeiro open. He cut the rope, freeing her ankle. Then he cut the rope binding her wrists to the saddle horn. He closed the knife.

She had moved to a discussion of his sexual habits in greater detail. He reached up and hauled her bodily out of the saddle. The girl slumped into him, hoping this feigned weakness would give her an advantage. Track held her at arm's length, looked briefly into her eyes to let her know he saw cunning there, then slapped her across the face. "You bitch," he snarled. "If you're crazy, I apologize. If you're not, I should kick you from here to Mexico instead of taking you there by horseback. See, I don't care that you liked El General. He was a viscious, scheming bastard. You wanna tell your daddy I killed El General, you tell him, but don't talk to me. You keep your mouth shut or I'll gag you and if that doesn't work I'll knock you unconscious. You like violence? It turns you on? Wonderful. You keep that filthy mouth going and you'll get violence you never dreamed possible. Understand me?"

Debbie turned from his stare and nodded.

Track swept her up in his arms and put her back on her horse. "Juan, tie her on. Make it quick." Track started back through the mud; the rain was heavier now he thought—if that were possible. He shot his arm from beneath the poncho and studied the black face of the Rolex for a moment. Then he turned to Maria. "How long till the border, you figure?"

"Three hours, Dan. A little less, perhaps."

Track nodded and, reaching his horse, remounted. He glanced back to the skinny Juan. "She set?"

"The *niña* is tied, Señor Track."

"Gracias," Track settled himself into the saddle. Then he looked at Maria and said, "Maybe I just will kill her." He grinned, digging his heels into the mud-splattered gray, and started ahead.

HIS REAR END ACHED; he imagined the horse wasn't too happy, either. In the past hour he had not dismounted at all, nor had he let the horse rest. The rain had stopped. That was why he spurred the animal ahead: with no rain the helicopters could get airborne again.

If Maria had been right, then two hours or less separated them from the border. And this Rodriguez guy would have to try something if he wanted the girl back. And as yet, nothing had happened. It had surprised him that the three helicopters had pulled back so easily, that they had not opened fire, even just as a scare tactic.

He could not shake the growing sense that he was riding into a trap.

When the rain had stopped he had brought the M-16 out from beneath his poncho. He carried it beneath his right arm now, slung cross body, the chamber loaded, a full 30-round magazine up the well. His eyes scanned the sky as he twisted his body in the saddle.

Where were they?

The girl had begun to talk again, but not to scream; there were no more obscenities, either. "You will all die, but I won't die. He will kill all of you, but he won't kill me. I'll beg him to keep me alive. So he won't kill me. I'll watch all of you die. They will probably rape you first, Maria, and make you take a very long time to die. And you, Mr. Track. Probably they'll beat you to death, or torture you over a fire. You will take a long time to die. But they already want me alive and I'll make them keep me alive. Lenny couldn't understand me—but this new colonel will understand me. El General understood me."

Track looked over his shoulder at the girl. To have shouted at her would have been useless. To have slapped her again might have made him feel better, at least for a time, but it would not have helped her.

He looked at Maria. She was making the sign of the cross and obviously praying, he didn't know for what. The Juans rode looking straight ahead, their faces blank. Debbie's prattle went on. "Debbie Hinchcliffe started all of this. She was jealous of Debbie Davis, jealous of me. I killed Debbie Hinchcliffe but they don't know it." She began to laugh.

Dan Track closed his eyes; maybe Maria had the right idea. Praying was about all they had left.

22

Track heard the sounds of the helicopters an instant before he heard the gunfire and saw its impact on the road surface along which they traveled. Digging his heels into the big gray, he shouted to Maria and the two Juans. "Run for it! They're coming!"

Gunfire erupted from the jungle to their left. Track leaned low across his horse's neck, the M-16 across the pommel of his saddle, and worked the selector to full-auto, firing blind into the jungle. He could only see muzzle-flashes and puffs of gray-white smoke in response and hear the pinging of assault-rifle rounds on the trail surface.

Debbie whooped with delight.

Track fired again into the foliage, this time hearing a shout of pain. He drew back tight on the reins, the gray rearing under him, as he looked skyward. The three helicopters were coming again. There were men running from the jungle now, firing M-16s. They were dressed in a motley assortment of fatigues and blue jeans, various handguns and knives festooned to their bodies. The terrorists—Rodriguez had got their loyalty somehow.

Track fired twice into the leading wedge of the terrorist onslaught, then whacked the rifle barrel against the flanks of his horse. The animal leaped ahead, Track clinging tightly to a handful of mane in the same fist as he held the reins.

Maria's big black was in the lead, almost seeming to fly, mane and tall out straight and rigid in the animal's own slipstream, Maria's shirt billowing up behind her. The skinny Juan's straw peasant hat blowing from his head.

More terrorist gunfire—then the fat Juan's body fell from the saddle. Track reined in. The helicopters were closing overhead, the voice of Rodriguez coming over a PA system, warning, "Surrender now or you will be killed!"

Track raised the second finger of his left hand skyward in the universal salute of contempt. He swung down from the saddle then, grasping the reins in his right fist. The animal seemed to scream at him, the whinnying sound high-pitched, unnerving, frightened.

Terrorists raced from the jungle now. Track fired toward them with the M-16 in his right fist, dropping to his knees beside the fat Juan. He was dead. Track fired out the rest of the M-16's 30-round stick as he fought to control the gray and vaulted up into the saddle. The animal was already moving as his feet found the stirrups and he settled himself in.

He let the empty rifle fall to his side on its sling, grabbing the waterlogged straw Stetson from his head and thwacking it against the animal's rump to urge it forward.

Gunfire. He felt a flash of pain, then a burning sensation in his left thigh. He looked down—a heavy crease from an assault rifle, blood spurting.

He lowered his body against the gray, his left hand finding the pressure point in the thigh to control the bleeding.

Debbie Hinchcliffe was still laughing.

From the helicopters overhead, small-arms fire hammered into the road surface around him. A massive gout of blood suddenly appeared on the gray's neck. The horse faltered for an instant, then recovered stride. Stupidly, Track had let himself become separated from Debbie Hinchcliffe. Now he was a target, the primary target he guessed.

He switched the reins to his bloodied left hand, finding his handerchief in his right hip pocket. It was one of the bandanna kind, that went with the cowboy clothes. Putting one end of it in his teeth, he began to twist it into a rope of cloth.

Low in the saddle now, the reins in his teeth, he bound the bandanna around his thigh, over the wound. He tied it tightly and took back the reins in both hands now. Mud splattered up around him. Suddenly the horse slipped, starting down. Track's arms encircled the animal's neck, urging the gray up and ahead.

Track was even now with Debbie. There was gunfire from behind him, from above and from the jungle to his left. Maria, her pistol in her left hand, turned, starting to shout something to Track. Suddenly the center of her beautiful face seemed to explode, fragments now floating in a cloud of blood as the body crumpled from the saddle.

"Maria!"

She was gone. Track reached out and grabbed at the loose reins of the black, dragging the animal with him, riding neck and neck beside Debbie. The skinny Juan's face was etched with panic, but he kept riding.

Rodriguez's voice sounded again. "You will all die—like the woman and the fat man. Surrender the girl and I will spare your lives!"

Juan stabbed a pistol skyward and fired. Retaliating gunfire rained down, stitching Juan's chest. His body lurched from the saddle, forcing Track's horse to jump to clear it.

"Shit," Track snarled.

The girl's horse reins were twisted onto the saddle horn of skinny Juan's mount and the animal, its eyes wide, bolted ahead.

Track reached to his soaked Levi's, grabbing for the Fazendeiro. Gunfire sprayed the track behind them now, but as long as he was close to the girl, Track knew the gunfire would come no nearer. Terrorists ran abreast of the horses now, firing pistols. From this gunfire he was not safe. He wondered if the terrorists really cared about keeping the girl alive.

He hacked at the reins of the girl's horse with the Fazendeiro. Finally the reins frayed and snapped. Track took the Fazendeiro and slashing it across the face and neck of one of the terrorists. He caught at the bridle of Debbie's horse before the animal could bolt. She wasn't laughing anymore.

Track reached down and cut her ankle free from the stirrup, drawing blood where he had missed with the knife.

Her wrists were still bound to the saddle horn. Track reached to her, chopping with the Fazendeiro's ample blade, again and again, the ropes snapping.

The girl shouted, "Asshole!" Both her hands knotted into the mane of the animal and she kicked the horse, sending it sprinting ahead.

Track dug his heels into the gray's flanks. He was gaining on Debbie when, from behind him, Track heard a new sound. He looked back. A jeep appeared with what could have been a Browning 50 mounted in the rear. The gun opened up, tearing chunks of dirt and rock from the ground near his horse's hooves. It *was* a Browning 50 from the sound of it.

He was even with the girl now. He reached for her and the girl's right hand flailed out toward him, her nails clawing at his face, just missing his left eye. Debbie was a bitch, but she was also his ticket out of this mess. He reached out and gave her an upper cut to the jaw. As Debbie went down, his left hand grabbed for her, bunching into her hair and the fabric of her dress at the shoulder. He hauled her out of the saddle and into the crook of his arm. The girl was only temporarily stunned. Her fists hammered at him, her nails clawed at him. Track fought to keep her pinned, his left arm around her, crossing from her left shoulder to the right side of her waist, his forearm between her breasts.

As her hands clawed at him, Track slammed his forehead against the side of her head to stun her. She sagged in his arm, semiconscious.

The Browning 50 was ripping chunks of the trail out from under him and the helicopter downdrafts ripped the straw cowboy hat from his head and lashed at his face.

Track kept riding.

Mexico couldn't be that far, he told himself.

The helicopter directly overhead was coming in low, making a pass, the gray edging away from it, the black tugging to be free of the reins.

Track hefted the semiconscious girl up, draping her across the gray's already lowered neck just in front of the saddle horn.

He held the reins in his left hand now, grasping the butt of the P-38 and ripping it from the sodden leather of the shoulder rig. He worked the safety off and fired toward the rotor blades. He heard a pinging sound, then the helicopter veered right.

Five rounds in his pistol as he counted it, his assault rifle empty, a she-wolf in front of him, the terrorists racing alongside him and the jeep with the Browning 50 behind him. Who knew what was in store for him on the second reel, Track thought.

He looked behind him, settling the P-38 as well as he could, aiming for the jeep's turned-down windshield and the driver behind it. He fired the last three rounds as rapidly as he could. The jeep suddenly lurched slamming into the rocks at the left side of the road, bouncing, jumping the ditch into the trees.

Track heeled into the gray.

Two helicopters overhead, neither of them firing.

Track slipped the P-38 into his waistband, his right fist knotting into the mane of the gray, the black tugging to be free.

The girl was beginning to stir. "Wonderful," Track muttered. He released the mane, the knife edge of his hand chopping downward, gently but firmly, against the side of the girl's neck. Her head slumped downward again. He had no time to fool with her.

Track reached for the knife with his left hand, taking both sets of reins in his right. He flicked it open one-handed, waved it in the air over his head, then brought it slowly toward the girl's throat.

He was gambling that the same ploy would work again.

He heard the voice of Rodriguez from one of the choppers. "If you kill the girl, your death shall be slow. You will beg for it!"

Track moved the knife closer to her throat, laying the flat of the blade against the carotid artery. If Rodriguez knew his stuff, he'd know what the knife could do.

"Do not harm her. We can make a deal."

Track kept the knife where it was, slowing the animal, outdistancing the terrorists now.

He brought the gray to a bone-jarring stop; the black started to rear, but Track was able to control it without moving the knife.

His left fist knotted in the girl's hair, drawing her head up to expose the throat more clearly. He wondered if he was bluffing, not really sure anymore.

Rodriguez shouted over the PA. "Let them go! Let them go!"

The terrorists fell back.

Track let her head fall, keeping the knife beside her throat. With his left arm he waved the helicopters back, the reins still in his left hand.

"You have won this round, *señor*. But you shall die. I promise that!"

The helicopters withdrew.

RODRIGUEZ SPOKE SLOWLY, Bastogne beside him, de Cristo, hands cuffed in front of his stomach, laughing. "Your men did no better than mine."

"My men, if you had not commanded them, would have killed the *norteamericano* and gotten the girl. So, you must have us invade Mexico now."

"Yes," Rodriguez whispered. "There is no other way for it. It is only a few miles before he reaches the border. And he will kill her if we try to stop him again. But once he is across the border, I do not think he would dare to kill her."

"And what if he does?" de Cristo asked.

"Then no one will have her."

De Cristo laughed again. "You are a fool, Rodriguez. And if you think I trust you, you are a bigger fool yet. My men will kill your assassin for you, then will get your girl. But she will not be handed over to you until I am handed over to my men."

Rodriguez thought for a moment, then nodded. "It is agreed."

"Your oath. You are fool enough to keep to it, I think," de Cristo declared, smiling.

"My oath. Just get the girl or you shall die. I also promise that."

De Cristo nodded. "Bring my lieutenants to me."

Rodriguez looked at Bastogne. "Go get them."

"And bring me a glass of whiskey. I am thirsty." De Cristo smiled.

"Bring him whiskey," Rodriguez snarled. Turning from Bastogne to de Cristo, he said, "You bring me the girl."

23

When the girl had awakened he had tied her on to the black horse. With some of his canteen water he had bathed the neck wound on the gray, it was a graze only and already had stopped bleeding. His own left thigh was much the same. It hurt a bit when he moved and the leg was stiffening slightly, but the wound wasn't serious. A flesh wound, as they say in the movies. What bothered him more was the prospect of getting a tetanus shot in Mexico. If he got to Mexico.

They were ridiculously close to the border now; if Rodriguez and his men came back, Track's only gambit would be to threaten the girl's life again. Since his name had not been used, there was no reason to suppose they knew who he was, and therefore no reason to assume they knew he would not kill the girl.

But once he was across the border, all that would change. Rodriguez could count on the terrorists crossing the border. And he could also count on Track not killing the girl now that he was so close to getting her out.

It was a rather ridiculous situation, Track thought. Once he crossed some magic invisible line, the rules of the game would change.

So far, the army, and the terrorists working with the army, had been heard from. He wondered if the Marseilles underworld people or the Mafia would become directly involved now.

He decided he had enough to worry about without looking for trouble.

As Track remounted the big gray he noticed that the girl was coming to.

"Hi, Debbie," Track greeted, smiling. "How's tricks, kid? Think of—" He was going to ask if she had thought of any new obscenities, but he thought better of it. There was no sense riding her, no sense provoking her. Things were tense enough already, there was no point making it worse. "Sorry I had to hit you," he told her.

She looked up at him and smiled. "Untie me and I'll screw your brains out, Track."

"Then what? Hit me over the head with a rock or something?"

"You don't trust me." She smiled.

That was an understatement, he thought. She was pretty in a reckless sort of way, and her blond hair, tangled from wind, wet still, enhanced the wild look in her eyes. The body wasn't bad; he'd had time to evaluate above the waist while she sat in Fuentes bed; her dress was bunched up to her hips as she straddled the black. "Let's put it this way," Track said, "I understand that you have some problems. That you're a little mixed up. And

I'm here to help you. The best way I can do that is to take you across the border, if we can get there. Some nice people who are really concerned about you—" that was sort of a lie, he thought "—are waiting to pick us up as soon as I place a phone call from a little village just over the border. You'll be in a warm bed by tonight, all clean, your hair combed. Safe, you'll have a better outlook on things."

"What's the matter? Can't you get it up?"

So much for that tactic. "Look, who's talking to me? Just so I know. Debbie Hinchcliffe or Debbie Davis?"

"I'm Debbie Davis. Debbie Hinchcliffe is dead."

"How'd Debbie Hinchcliffe die?"

"I killed her."

"Right—" Track nodded "—you bet." He swung up onto his horse. "Right." The summit of the mountain ahead was the start of Mexico. Just Mexico, he hoped, and nothing else.

"WE SHOULD BE HEARING from Major Track at any time now, sir. And we can send out the chopper. But there are some problems." Fernando Murphy took a cigar from the pocket of his aloha shirt and began to remove the cellophane.

"What's the problem?" the man he was unaccustomed to dealing with asked from across his desk in the small office in the building three blocks from the White House.

"Well, apparently Track killed or had a hand in killing Ignacio Fuentes."

"That's fuckin' wonderful," the man Murphy didn't particularly like said.

"Yeah, well, and there's this other thing."

"What?"

"The girl. We did a little digging to find out if there was anything that needed to be covered up. We found a real lulu."

"What?"

"She's got this other name she uses—right? Debbie Davis?"

"I know that."

"And she had this girl—this Angela Coin—taking her classes for her, under the name Debbie Hinchcliffe?"

"So? The girl should be easy enough to convince that she's doing her country a service by keeping her mouth shut. We can even arrange an incentive for her if that'll help. Check it out and let me know."

"The girl won't talk—ever," Murphy said.

"The girl is dead?"

"The girl was murdered and everything points to Debbie Hinchcliffe as her killer."

"Why?"

"Well, while she was Debbie Davis, she seemed to talk like she knew Debbie Hinchcliffe and hated her."

"So?"

"So, Debbie is a nut case. At least that's what my people figure. She killed Debbie Hinchcliffe herself, that is—in the person of Angela Coin. Slashed Angela Coin with a straight razor looks like. Or maybe some kinda butcher knife. Not enough left intact that you could really tell it was a person. She's a sickie—real bad."

"Great. And she's the daughter of an important U.S. senator—at least he thinks he's important."

"Yes, sir. So, ah, I was wondering. You know. I have some contacts down there. It's not as if Track didn't get her out of the hands of Fuentes and the mob people and all. If he contacts us—"

"You're about to make a suggestion I have no interest in hearing," the man across the desk interrupted. "But I believe you to be a man with a great deal of personal initiative. And therefore I trust your judgment. Leave me now." The man swiveled his chair toward the window and turned his face down toward a sheaf of papers in a manila file.

Fernando Murphy stood up, pulling his shirttail over his gun. "You bet, sir. Just never throw this at me or you're dead. He turned from the desk and walked away. A pay phone would be the best bet—and there was one outside the building.

He wondered how much change he could get out of the newspaper stand downstairs without making it so the guy would remember him.

He decided to try a different phone.

HE FOUND A PHONE in a small restaurant going out toward Maryland, where the neighborhood wasn't so bad that he couldn't leave his car. It took three tries on the pay phone—three beers and a hamburger and a half-eaten piece of apple pie—before he got the man he wanted. He could speak frankly with the man. "Ralph? Fernando. How ya been?"

"Fine, Fernando. What's up?"

Murphy looked over his shoulder, no one seemed to be paying attention to him and the bar was too dark for a lip-reader. "I got a problem. We sent a guy named Dan Track down into, well—"

Ralph mentioned the name of the country.

"You got it."

"Figured that when Fuentes went down. Bout time, too."

"Yeah, well, that wasn't the reason we sent Track in there, ya know. American girl—"

"Hinchcliffe, Deborah Louise."

"You're well informed."

"Gotta be, Fernando," the voice came back cheerily through the phone.

Fernando Murphy felt anything but cheery. "The girl turns out to be whacko. A killer. Instead of picking her up north of that little place you mentioned like we'd arranged, we want something else. Can you do it?"

"The man, too?"

"Yeah," Murphy agreed, nodding. It was too bad, but Track wasn't the kind of guy who'd keep his mouth shut.

"Sure. How much?"

"How should I know how much. I never done this before."

"I have. You want I should tell you?" Ralph asked.

Murphy laughed. "So tell me."

"Twenty-five thousand apiece."

"What do you mean? For you and everybody you use?

"No. Jeez, man. What do you think I am? A gouger or something. No, a head—the girl and this Track guy."

"I think that can be arranged." It had damn well better be, Murphy thought. It was too late to back out now.

"How good is the guy?"

"Very good. Why the hell you think we picked him in the first place?"

"Well, I'm just checking, you know. How many guys, what kind of equipment? You were going to pull him, right?"

"Right."

"When was he gonna contact you?"

A mechanical operator—a recording—broke in and asked for more change. Murphy fed the phone, the mechanical voice thanking him. "Anytime beginning tonight. There's a phone number he has."

"I'd say let him call it and we can be waiting there for him. Where's the phone?"

"How's your Spanish?"

"Good. How's yours?"

"Classify Matthew, Mark, Luke and John in their relationship to our Holy Mother the church, and you got it."

"All right, I got it. When do I get the ah..."

"As soon as I get it and figure out a way for you to get it. Look, thanks for not makin' this worse, Ralph."

"I understand, Fernando. I really do. Be seein' ya." The phone clicked dead.

Murphy held the phone for a few more seconds, pretending to talk into it. He was almost afraid to hang up.

24

Ralph Melon always kept a plane ready to go. He was, after all, very much involved in a business where lightning-fast decisions had to be made and acted upon. And he had called the airport as soon as he had gotten off the telphone with Fernando Murphy.

It amused him—a man of the law requiring his services. But he had been amused in similar ways before. That was how he had met Murphy. Murphy had attempted to arrest him and been told not to.

Life was complicated, he reflected, pushing the button that slid the bookcase aside to reveal the safe door.

He began working the combination. If this man Track was very good, then three extra people would give Ralph ample margin.

He swung open the safe door.

His most precious things, aside from his family, of course, were housed there.

Money. He took down a stack of twenties and then another. He considered for a moment. He took a third stack.

He was giving Murphy a bargain—fifty thousand for two hits. But, patriotism always softened his heart. He was not blind to the nature of his profession. But he felt, too, that it was times such as these that, however slightly, redeemed him.

He was serving his country, and that was a good feeling for any man. Serving in a way few could.

Definitely three packs of twenties.

Between Los Angeles and Mexico there would not be any problems. He would fly in and fly out and never land until he reached the little town. Between calls he had checked the map.

Los Quantros Santos. He took his own special gun from the safe. There was one in the desk drawer of course, and one in the nightstand beside the bed for his wife to have available when he was away. But not a gun like this. This gun was very special. It had been stolen by his son in Vietnam. He felt a thrill of pride thinking of his son's service to his country against the commies. The commies were bastards, he thought, and he had said so on numerous occasions.

His son had smuggled the gun back a piece at a time. One of the original stainless-steel Smith and Wesson autos in 9 mm, before the production of stainless pistols, even before the Model 59. The first Smith auto with the double-column magazine feature. It was one of what had been rumored at the time to be perhaps two dozen guns made for use by special commando teams, hand built, fitted with a special silencer and a slide lock. The supply of subsonic ammo his son had smuggled back had not gone far, but Ralph Melon had found a very skilled man to manufacture more of it for him. The ballistics and the group size of the new stuff was better than the original.

He hefted the very special Smith and Wesson.

Bradford James Melon, his son, had died two weeks before the fall of Saigon. Perhaps this Track fellow was a commie, perhaps not. But an enemy of his country he would kill.

He took the solitary spare magazine and the box of forty rounds of the custom ammo made for him without a head stamp. The silencer had recently been refurbished.

Ralph liked the justice of it. He would hit this man his government wanted killed with the gun that his dead son had given him.

He closed the safe door.

25

Track patted the neck of his horse as he watched the sun set to his right beyond the mountains. To his left purple darkness filled the valley below. Ahead was Mexico. Behind him—he wanted to forget that.

His palms sweated slightly. That Rodriguez would try something seemed more likely by the instant.

In the past hour or so the girl had been pleasant—quite pleasant. He wondered if she was relaxing now that her ordeal was almost over and was coming back to normal.

The girl interrupted his thoughts. "I promise I won't try to get away, Mr. Track. Dan, isn't it?"

"Yeah, Debbie—Dan. Look. I'm sure your intentions are good but what if... Well, you'll be better off when I get you to the people who love you."

"Why won't you love me?"

He answered her honestly. "I've got a girl. I mean, it's not that you aren't attractive. But she doesn't cheat on me, so I don't cheat on her."

"She's very lucky."

Track smiled at her, spontaneously this time. "Thank you. That's a nice thing to say. Now you just hang in there, Debbie, and everything'll be fine."

"If you say so, Dan. I get—well, I get these terrible headaches and then I say and do things that...I don't even remember all of it, sometimes."

Track reached out to hold her hands, her wrists still bound to her saddle horn. "It'll be all right. I won't let anybody hurt you. And before you know it, you'll be your old self again, Debbie. Honest." He squeezed her hands.

"Can I kiss you?"

Track looked at her. "You don't have to do that," he almost whispered. "I'd like to kiss you. Like two friends."

"All right," Track leaned closer to her. Her lips parted slightly as her head arched back. Track touched his mouth to hers; her lips were moist, warm. She wasn't trying to sex him, he thought. It was just a nice kiss, friendly, like she had said.

"I'm glad you're helping me," she told him. "I like you."

"Thank you." He didn't lie and say he liked her back. He wanted to like her and hoped she would let him. "Come on. We have to be careful. This Rodriguez guy probably sent his terrorists after us. So stick with me and do just as I say."

"All right, Dan, I will. I promise I will." She smiled again. There was something like a twinge of pain visible in her eyes.

"What's the matter?"

"My wrists—they hurt a little. But you're right. Don't untie me. I might, well, the headaches might start again."

"I can loosen...."

"No, if it hurts real bad I'll tell you."

"All right." Track took the reins of his own horse and hers more firmly in his right hand and started down the other side of the mountain.

BASTOGNE FELT VERY UNCOMFORTABLE. He was in Mexico, illegally, with twenty-five of de Cristo's terrorists, a half dozen of Rodriguez's men and Rodriguez himself. He climbed down from the jeep and stared along the single street of Los Quatros Santos. "Talk about a one-horse town. I do not think this town even has one horse," he joked, laughing, trying to cover his own fear. Rodriguez was beside him now. "*Mon ami*, what do you think? Have you ever seen a smaller town?"

"And this town will be even smaller, soon." Rodriguez started to laugh, as though at some private joke, then walked down the street, two of his six men with him, flanking him. Bastogne fell in after them.

It had apparently not rained here. With the sun setting the white of the brick-and-frame buildings that lined both sides of the street, most of them single-story and some with false fronts, seemed yellow and red.

Rodriguez called to the terrorist leader de Cristo had appointed. "Take six men. Find the mayor of this stinking piss-pot town and bring him to me, along with his family."

"*Sí*, Colonel," the man said, nodding, calling to some of his men, taking off in a run ahead of Rodriguez along the street.

RUDY WATCHED, HIS FIST TIGHT on the wooden grips of the Bolo Mauser, the safety off, a round chambered already but the hammer lowered. He had one of the safeties that predated the universal safety, he had read a book about Mauser pistols once. With the safety pushed up alongside the hammer, the hammer strut was pushed rearward slightly and the gun wouldn't fire. His safety had been moved downward, horizontal to the line of the frame.

He could see seven men in what appeared to be military fatigues. Two of his own four men were with him in the boarded-up cafè, as well as six of the Mexicans Mr. Halston had supplied.

His other two men and the other four Mexicans were across the street and down, using the shed between the stable and the church.

Rudy licked his lips.

These guys were evidently terrorists—since they weren't Mexican army. Of that he was reasonably certain.

They were armed with M-16s and a motley-looking assortment of handguns and knives—if the six runners, the only ones he could see in detail, were at all typical.

He was glad for the SPAS 12s and the Uzis, glad for his own M-16s. He didn't doubt the professionalism of the Mexicans, he had worked with people from their organization before. And he didn't doubt the professionalism of his own boys.

Mr. Halston, standing beside him, whispered, "Rodriguez."

"Sir?"

"Fuentes's number-one boy—Rodriguez—he musta taken over. And that's Bastogne with him."

Rudy peered farther down the street through the crack in the boards. He was grateful for the foresight that had caused him to remove the glass from the window, otherwise they would have been suffocating in the cantina. "I'm not sure I understand, sir. Are these..."

"These guys are here to meet their boy to get the girl from him. Shit—I never expected this."

"Why wouldn't they meet him in their own country, sir? Why here?"

"How the hell do I know?" Halston snarled.

"What do we do?"

"Smoke the bastards, what do you think?"

"Yes, sir," Rudy replied, nodding, "but can I suggest that we wait until their triggerman gets here with the girl. If we start shooting now, well, we just might scare them off."

"You got a good head on your shoulders, Rudy." Halston clapped him on the shoulder. "You're the general. You done this sorta thing a lot more than me. Yeah, we'll wait then. But remember this, if it's at all possible, I get Bastogne myself. And we don't kill Rodriguez."

Rudy licked his lips again. Despite the cool shirt made of loosely woven cotton that his wife had packed for him, he was still warm.

He shrugged. Being comfortable wasn't one of the requirements of his job.

26

Track could see the one-street, perhaps twenty-building town clearly, at the very beginning of the valley at the base of the mountains. He lowered the binoculars. He thought about Maria Sanchez—dead. The fat Juan, the skinny Juan—both dead. The DEA man, Cheatum—dead.

There had been no sign of the enemy. Neither terrorists nor government troops. He looked up at Debbie from where he stood now beside her horse, his straw Stetson low over his eyes against the sun. "That's the town, Debbie."

"It looks desolate," she observed, smiling.

"I'm going to untie your hands and your ankle. If we get down there and Roriguez and his people are waiting for us, you might have to make a run for it yourself. Twenty-five miles or so north of here, well, there's a good-size town and they should have cops. If anything goes down here, I'll try and hold 'em as long as I can. That black's a good horse. If you don't burn him out, he'll get you the twenty-five miles."

"But you'd be dead," she whispered.

"Yeah. You get outa here and I don't get yourself to a Telex and, well, just try Desiree. Tell her...Desiree—well—just tell her, okay?'' Track smiled at the girl as he cut her ankle free, then started to cut the ropes binding her hands to the saddle horn. She flexed her fingers, slowly at first, then started to pull off the gloves they had put over her hands. She smiled down at him.

''Do you think they're waiting for us?''

''Yeah, I think so. But I can't risk the extra twenty-five miles because they'd get us for sure. In the desert there isn't any place to hide.''

''Can I dismount for a minute?''

''Sure.'' Track reached up to help her down from the saddle.

She laughed, ''Panties aren't made to cushion your rear end in the saddle.'' She rubbed at her behind as though it were sore, and she laughed again.

''This has been hard on you, I know,'' Track told her.

He still had the Fezendeiro open. The one he had back home had been imported from Brazil by B & D Trading Company and was the largest of their knives. This one was Brazilian, as well; he wondered how it had gotten from the hands of the Resistance to El General. He shrugged it off, beginning to cut away the remnants of rope on the girl's saddle horn as she talked. ''It's too bad you and I never were able to get it on, Mr. Track—Dan.''

Track found himself smiling. ''Well, truth to tell, honey, either you're a little young for me or I'm a little old for you. But don't think I wasn't flattered.'' He had the last of the rope cut. As he started to turn around he saw the rock in her hands as it hammered toward his head.

AFTER HE FELL she hit him on the head with the rock two more times. Then she dropped the rock. It bounced in the dirt beside his head and she watched as blood trickled from his left temple in tiny rivulets. Blood smeared the front of his forehead, as well.

She dropped to her knees in the sand beside him and pried his fingers from the knife and picked it up. She stared at it. The blade had a funny shape. She had no idea how to close it.

The knife she had used to kill that snooty bitch Debbie Hinchcliffe—to cut her pretty face to pieces, to cut her breasts—it had been a butcher knife taken from Lenny's kitchen. She had returned it to the drawer after washing it with dishwashing liquid in his sink. She had burned the plastic bag she had carried the knife in.

Debbie Davis studied the face of Dan Track. It was a handsome face. The mustache accentuated the bone structure. He was well tanned. Tall, good-looking, strong, tough—the kind of guy a lot of women would fall out of their panties for. She smiled and pressed the blade of his big shinny pocketknife to his neck. She watched as a tiny fleck of blood appeared. It would be so easy, she laughed.

Then she started to laugh more loudly. She reached down to his zipper, opening the fly of his Levi's. She undid the trophy buckle. She muttered to herself, "Men make it so hard to get into their pants. Like they're guarding something important." The buckle undone, she opened the metal button at the waist and spread the pants front open wide. If she cut it off, he'd never wake up. He would never know that she did it. It wouldn't be like killing Debbie Hinchcliffe. Debbie had been awake while she'd been cut, mutilated.

Debbie Davis sat back on her haunches. She had to let him know.

She inserted the knife under his scrotum and left it there. He'd know she could have.

She stood up, putting her left foot on his chest, and with both hands pulled the pistol from his shoulder holster.

The things usually had some kind of safety, and she assumed it was the thing on the left side at the top. She pointed the gun at his abdomen, gently squeezing the trigger. The trigger pulled back only part way and nothing happened.

She worked the thing that she thought might be the safety, then still pointing the gun at Track, she started to pull the trigger again. This time she could feel the pressure.

She put the safety back on.

She started away from him, taking the fallen reins of the big black horse, cooing to it gently, then mounting. She had always been a good horsewoman. She had learned to ride at the same place Debbie Hinchcliffe had. She had done a lot with Debbie.

As she turned the animal, bringing it under control, she looked at Dan Track, unconscious in the dust, his face bleeding, the knife at his crotch. "You missed the best lay in the world, Track," she jeered, laughing.

If Rodriguez was waiting in the village, he would take her back and use her like El General had used her.

If he wouldn't she'd use the gun to kill Rodriguez—and maybe kill Debbie Davis, too.

27

Dan Track didn't open his eyes. As he started to move, his whole head screamed with the pain. And something felt strange at his crotch.

He tried to open his eyes. The left eye wouldn't open; it was encrusted with something. He decided it was probably blood. He raised his head a little, then let it sink back, tremors of pain seizing him. He moaned. Knowing what to expect now, he slowly raised himself up on his elbows.

His knife was open and laid out beneath his scrotum, the blade upward, as though to cut...

He shuddered; it was not the pain but the thought.

He reached forward and down, gently removing the knife and dropping it to the ground beside him.

He rolled left and up onto his knees and hands. His head was at once detached and a horrible part of him.

He sat back on his haunches waiting for the dizziness to pass, bending his head forward, his hands fumbling to stuff his shirt back in, to close his pants. "Bitch," he hissed through his teeth.

He got her message; she could have done it to him, but didn't because he would never have awakened, would never have known it. "Damn you," he groaned, falling forward as he closed his belt.

Track pushed himself forward; the gray was standing there. He reached out with his left hand to the left stirrup, grabbing it; the horse moving away a little, dragging him. "Whoa, take it easy," he whispered.

His right hand found the fender above the stirrup, and he started to pull himself up. His left hand moved along the fender and over the seat to the horn as he pulled himself to his full height, then sagged against the saddle.

Leaning his head against the saddle, he groped with his left hand for the canteen, hoping she hadn't taken it from him, half surprised she had left the horse.

Track found the strap for the canteen and began to unwind it from the horn. He leaned heavily against the animal, praying the gray—Cuchillo was its name—would not move.

He uncapped the canteen, raising his head slowly to drink.

The canteen water tasted as bad as he had remembered it, but at least he had every reason to suspect it was clean.

He closed his eyes, recapping the canteen, resting.

AFTER SOME TIME—he didn't really know how long but darkness had long since fallen—he had used his lighter and the metal shaving mirror from his saddlebags to inspect his wounds. The leg, where he had been grazed by the bullet, oddly wasn't bothering him. The center of his forehead was abraded and skinned, but there was only surface bleeding and although the wound stung as he did it, the caked blood washed away easily. The back of his head ached badly; after swabbing at it with a damp rag, no fresh blood appeared there, either. His left temple still bled and he took a damp bandanna handkerchief and tied it over the wound. There was a deep cut on his cheek. He started to laugh at himself: if he had to blow his nose, he'd be out of luck.

He wasn't thinking clearly, he realized, but at least he was thinking.

It was then that he realized the P-38 was gone. His rifle still hung from his saddle horn. Either the girl had missed it or hadn't bothered.

She was a good rider; as best he could piece together the time of these events, unless she had run the black out, she wouldn't have reached Los Quatros Santos quite yet. She would have taken the road, the sensible way to get there if, like Debbie, you wanted to be recaptured.

His head ached, but at least it kept him awake. He was having little difficulty evaluating the bad news in the situation, but the good news was more difficult. There didn't seem to be any.

He could forget about her and take the gray up into the rocks, find a comfortable spot to make a fireless camp and sleep through the night. No one would be looking for him once the girl was found.

Then he could skirt around Los Quatros Santos and ride the twenty-five miles or so across the desert to the next town and get himself taken out.

He had three loaded thirties, one of them in the M-16 already. And there was a round in the chamber. Ninety-one rounds and the Fazendeiro.

Likely the village would be swarming with terrorists.

He shrugged his shoulders. It hurt when he shrugged his shoulders.

Dan Track hoped they hadn't cut the wires on the phone. He began to check the cinch strap on his saddle. Where was George when he really needed him?

28

Debbie had found a sharp stick to use to pry the stone from the black's hoof. The animal would be fine to ride—in a few days. She had loosed the cinch, removed the saddle and the bridle, and left the horse.

The village could not be too far now, she reassured herself. As she walked on in the dark she thought of Dan Track. He had probably come to by now and found the little surprise she had left for him. She laughed at that. Mr. Macho—almost Mr. Eunuch.

If he had the strength to get up, he'd probably have the brains to stay back up in the mountains.

She walked along, the P-38 in her right hand, held almost lazily, her left hand toying with the mud-stained skirt of her once-blue dress.

She thought about Maria Sanchez—it was Maria's dress.

She thought of Debbie Hinchcliffe. What a spoiled bitch, she thought. Debbie Hinchcliffe's father had given her money, given her riding lessons and skiing lessons, given her, given her. She almost felt sorry for Debbie Hinchcliffe. Maybe Debbie was better off dead. Debbie Hinchcliffe's father had given her things but had never talked to her, had never given her love. Debbie Hinchcliffe was better off dead.

Her thoughts shifted; she wondered if Rodriguez would be like Fuentes. Or could she get him to be? Fuentes wouldn't have hit her if he hadn't cared for her. Track had hit her, too, but that was different.

She wondered what Track's woman was like. Closer to his age, probably. More like Debbie Hinchcliffe. If that was the kind of woman Track wanted, she was almost sorry she hadn't used the knife.

As Debbie Davis hugged her hands to her upper arms to ward off the chill of the new night, she began to plan what she would do. She would go to Rodriguez, get down on her knees to him. That would make him feel good. She wondered what he looked like. She began fantasizing about that. Would he be rougher with her than Fuentes had been to punish her for escaping? It wasn't her fault, but she was sure he would punish her anyway. And if he punished her, it would show that he loved her.

As she contemplated what he might do to her she felt her body grow warm in the chilly night.

TRACK HAD NOT TAKEN THE ROAD down along the mountain; instead, half the time leading the gray, unable to ride because of the ruggedness of the terrain, he had started down cross-country, planning to intersect the road just before it entered the village. Perhaps he would intersect the path taken by

Debbie Hinchcliffe. If he got the girl out—prospects for success were admittedly dim—she would be hospitalized for a long time, he theorized. He had never studied psychology in depth, but it didn't take an expert to know the girl was very sick.

Split personality, he supposed. There were some fascinating cases on record that he had read about in popular literature. Two personalities—one hating the other. No one had told him that Debbie was mentally disturbed. He wondered how far she would go? She had nearly killed him—with intent. That he was still alive was not her fault. He likely had a concussion—already he had suffered a wave of nausea and had had to stop for several minutes. She had tried to murder him. And the thing with the knife. Not exactly a girlish prank. He did not consider himself someone who had led a sheltered life, but Debbie's warped message had shocked him.

He attributed it to her mental condition, of course. No doubt, if she was someday restored to health and were to remember it, it would likely shock her more than it shocked him.

The incline eased into a flat expanse, and he remounted the gray, urging it ahead, but slowly. That the animal was sure-footed had been proven to him along the muddy trails heading up into the mountains, but when the clouds scudded between the mountainside and the moon, it was very dark—too dark. He reined the animal back so it would travel as slowly as possible.

He began to formulate a plan.

If Debbie reached the village before him, which he had no doubt she would, considering the speed at which he was forced to travel now, he would circle the village and enter from the far side. It wouldn't be hard to spot Rodriguez and his men, or the terrorists, or both. He could work his way to wherever Debbie would be held, then play it by ear from there.

If he could reach the telephone—it was supposedly located in the mayor's home—he could perhaps call in for help. That sort of thing always worked in movies and books. A squad of CIA commandos or something would arrive in the nick of time to save the day. Not likely, but there was the Mexican federal police.

The way his luck was running of late, the helicopter that was to pick him up would break down, or the mayor's telephone would be out of order.

RUDY EDGED ALONG THE SIDE of the cantina, the Bolo Mauser tight in his right fist. He had left Halston and the others to reconnoiter on their own, and left more bulky equipment behind him, as well. Only little Broomhandle—a smile crossed his lips. It was, after all, small for a broom handle.

Rudy was afraid, and he focused his mind elsewhere to eliminate the fear, a trick he had learned years ago. In the old days it had been baseball stats, football plays and girls. He had stopped thinking about girls other than his wife the day he had met her. But baseball stats and football plays still interested him. But now he thought about his pistol. It would have been simpler over the years to move to something modern. The stripper clips were a perennial problem although at present he had a sufficient supply. The ammo was sometimes difficult, too, but for now having it custom-made wasn't too much of a problem. In a pinch, there was always the 7.62 Tokarev ammo—that had come in handy on a few jobs, using the Mauser and leaving Soviet-type cases behind. A little confusion never hurt. Occasionally, he just left the Bolo Mauser at home and used a Beretta 9 mm or a Walther or some other gun instead. But the Bolo was his weapon of choice, and his right palm sweated on the serrated wooden grips now. It felt like a broom handle—hence the name.

The moon was partially behind clouds, giving enough light for him to see, but he hoped, not to be seen.

The terrorists or whomever they were, were in hiding throughout the far end of the village, and Rudy had silently wondered who the rather obese man had been that had been brought to the one called Colonel Rodriguez. He assumed the mayor of the town, if a town this size had a mayor.

With the fat man had been an attractive woman in her late thirties; clinging to her skirts had been three children, ages ranging from ten or eleven to about five. Rudy was a good judge of children's ages—he had his own and that was the best training.

From the far end of the cantina overlooking the street, he could see no movement. No villagers had appeared on the streets since the terrorists had arrived. Lights were on and the smell of cooking fires was faint on the air. It was a very primitive place, but it had a certain charm, he thought absently. Everyone was indoors because everyone was afraid.

He didn't like fear, although sometimes he had used it.

He considered how best to cross the street. As the night had progressed it had gotten gradually cooler and now his black Windbreaker covered his cream-colored shirt, and he wore dark slacks and dark shoes. He watched the moon. A dead run when the clouds completely obscured the moon might do the trick. There were no terrorists this far along the street.

He waited. He watched.

The clouds moved and Rudy ran, the Bolo in his right hand, the safety off, ten rounds loaded.

There was a long, low building, apparently a stable, across the street from the cantina and he aimed himself toward it, running as fast and as quietly as he could. The sound of the gravel and sand beneath his feet was as loud as gunshots to him, but he hoped that was just one of those little tricks fear played on you.

Rudy sagged beside the wall of the stable, leaning his face against the splotchy stuccolike covering of the adobe, sweating.

There had been no gunfire. Therefore, he had not been seen—he hoped.

Suddenly, at the end of the street, he saw movement. A girl. She was alone. There was something in her hand—maybe a gun. He couldn't be certain. But she was alone. Rudy's mind raced; maybe the Marseilles guy was being clever, sending her in on her own in case it was a trap. Rudy smiled at that. Two traps? He wasn't as certain as Halston was that the Rodriguez guy and the others were waiting for the Marseilles shooter with open arms.

And why a girl with a gun? It could have been empty, but still—

Rudy edged closer to the corner of the wall, the Bolo raised, the safety off still. Figures came from out of the shadows—terrorists or soldiers or whatever they were, but from where the girl walked, down the center of the street, she was not able to see them. If they didn't stop her, he could grab her.

He waited; the timing was critical. The wrong move could get her killed, him killed.

He would rely on the moon again; run into the street, get the gun from her and drag her to the cantina.

It would mean a shootout, but he judged his own men better equipped than the guys in the strange uniforms, and probably better trained; it might make up for the fact that the odds were slightly stacked in favor of the other guys.

He watched the moon and waited.

It was definitely a gun in the girl's hand, looked like a P-38, but she held it awkwardly, as though she didn't know how to hold it at all.

She looked dirty, tired, and there was something funny about her face. The set of her eyes was off.

She was too far away for him to see her eyes themselves, but something was wrong.

He watched the moon, his trouser pockets packed with loaded 10-round stripper clips. He began to sweat. Suddenly the Windbreaker was too hot. He knew the fear was starting.

She was almost even with him now, the shadowy figures from the other end of the street moving into the open. Then the moon was lost behind the clouds again.

Rudy ran toward the girl. He heard a shout from the end of the street. The girl started to turn around but stopped as soon as she saw him. She raised the pistol and fired, the muzzle-flash blindingly bright in the darkness. "Shit," Rudy muttered as he dodged right.

There was another shout from the end of the street. Rudy could see them, but didn't know if they could see him.

The girl was getting ready to fire again. Rudy stormed toward her, throwing a body block against her, knocking her to the street. As he rolled onto his back, he spread his legs, settled the Bolo downrange and fired three times, the sharp cracks of the 7.63 Mauser rounds earsplitting in the stillness.

Then he was up, retrieving the Walther from the sand and stuffing it into his belt, grabbing the girl by the hair and dragging her to her feet. "Come on, lady," he snarled.

More shouting, then gunfire from the end of the street.

Someone shouted something in Spanish that was close enough to Italian that Rudy recognized it. "Pepe, he is dead now?"

Another reason for Rudy to carry the Bolo—he was good with it.

He quick-marched the girl toward the cantina. She fought him all the way, screaming obscenities and trying to claw at him.

Rudy was old-fashioned when it came to women and dirty talk. He yanked and threw her up the curb to the wooden sidewalk, splintering now under a rain of assault-rifle fire.

Rudy dived through the bat-wing doors of the cantina after her. The men around him opened fire into the street. The men across the street ceased fire as they had been ordered to.

Rudy lay on the floor a minute, catching his breath.

Halston was dragging the girl to her feet, laughing. "Damn it, Rudy. You're good."

Rudy didn't reply. He already knew that.

29

Track was close enough now that the field glasses were a matter of convenience rather than necessity. He had left the gray unsaddled, tied up in a grove of cottonwoods just to the south of the village. If for some reason he didn't make it back, after a time the animal would likely be able to get free.

He could see the flashes of gunfire, hear the sounds. Assault rifles, pistols, riot shotguns—each had its own peculiar pitch. The shotguns had the familar sound of a SPAS. He'd made that particular music often himself to recognize it.

Troops were running from one end of the street to the other. When the clouds cleared the moon he could see troops forming by a long low buiding—a stable, he guessed, or perhaps a chicken house.

As he watched, gunfire started near a church, which was up the street from the stable. The troops were in a cross fire.

He saw no sign of the girl.

And another peculiar thing—just before the gunfire began in the village, he could have sworn he heard the sound of a powerful twin-engine plane, but there had been no running lights.

If the girl was not already in the village, she would not be foolish enough to enter it now. If she was here, the people in the building at the far end of the village would have her, and the troops now caught in the cross fire would want her.

He wondered what the plane had to do with it all.

The most logical course, other than staying out of it entirely, seemed to be to get down into the village and somehow get into the building that had originally come under fire. He would have to do it before the troops—Rodriguez's men or the terrorists or both, he couldn't be certain—thought of the same thing and sent personnel to approach the contested building from the rear.

He had discarded the cowboy hat when it wouldn't fit over his bandanna bandage and had donned the GI surplus M-51 field jacket that had been in with his bedroll. He shrugged out of the jacket now; his shirt was darker than the jacket. Carrying the M-16, he started down from the rocks, toward the village; the gunfire was more sporadic now, as though everyone was trying to figure out what to do next.

Track quickened his pace.

Track stopped; it was the sound of a voice. A lull in the gunfire made it audible. Slowly Track flattened himself to the ground, holding his breath, listening.

Two voices, at least. From the plane, he realized.

It could have been help, sent in by his own government when he had not called from the village. But it was too soon for that. Since there was no way of telling if they were his own people or not, he couldn't gamble that they were.

He waited, listening. Any thought that these men were on his side disappeared immediately. One man said, "This Track guy, they say how he was armed, Mr. Melon?"

"No. But probably not too good. Don't sweat it."

"Right," the voice answered.

Track rolled slowly, easily onto his back, the pain in his head somehow distant from him now. He kept listening as he stared toward the clouds that alternately exposed and obscured the moon. Melon, he thought, trying to remember. Damn this headache. Then it came to him.

"Melon," he said under his breath. Ralph Melon. It was one of those books put out by some of the small publishers, one of those things that names names, places, dates, a book that isn't really a book but an indictment. The people mentioned in those books never sue; the publicity from the suit would only make the book sell more copies and further destroy the reputations of those named in it.

Who had had the book? He tried to remember. A young captain he had worked with just before leaving CID. The guy had been a budding journalist, wanting to get into investigative reporting. He read books like that all the time. Track closed his eyes, listening for the voices, but at the same time recalling other voices.

He had gone into Captain Julius Albright's office and sat down.

"Major, what's up?"

"Nothin', Julie. Just wanted to see if you got anything more on those guys who were trying to sell the porno flicks on base?"

"One of the guys I interviewed—he was real eager to cooperate, Major, once I told him what he was facing for buying the stuff. He said there was a woman in it. A blonde. I'm talkin' with the other buyers this afternoon to get some more dope on the woman."

Track had nodded, turning around the jacketless book on Albright's desk. "More exposés?"

"Hey, Major. This is good. A fella named Ralph Melon."

"Any relation to watermelon?"

"I'm serious, Major. You should read about this guy—an assassin."

Track had borrowed the book a few days later, read it in an evening, and returned it.

Ralph Melon. Purportedly in some kind of special branch of the OSS during World War II. All the people in it did was kill behind enemy lines. After the war, Melon had been twenty-one—that would put him close to sixty, Track guessed, if it was the same Melon. And Melon had been so good at what he did he kept doing it—for everybody except the Communists. Melon was a patriot. Killing for the mob, for other people who needed death, was okay according to Melon's code, but anything anti-American was evil. Track remembered the last chapter of the book. Melon's youngest child, his only son, had been in Special Forces in Vietnam.

The boy had been killed. The last chapter had tried—not too successfully as Track remembered it—to link Melon to the shooting deaths of three North Vietnamese officials in Ho Chi Minh City two months after the cease-fire. The three North Vietnamese officials had all been involved with the other side of the operation during which Melon's boy had died in combat.

He couldn't blame Melon for that. It was the sort of thing Track would have done if someone had killed his son.

But the book had never mentioned Melon doing any work for the government that didn't involve termination.

Suddenly Track knew why Ralph Melon was walking down the trail on the other side of the rocks.

The girl, Ralph Melon, all of it, fit very nicely together.

Either Track was delerious from the knock on the head or he was finally seeing things clearly.

He had the sick feeling it was the latter.

Ralph Melon had been sent to kill him.

Track's hands tightened on the M-16. He had tied the sling swivels with scraps of leather from the bottom of the saddlebags, apparently left there for emergency harness repairs. The gun was silent—until it went off.

Track rose slowly, into a crouch. The voices were even with his position now on the other side of the rocks.

Going against Ralph Melon, even at age sixty or so, was like going against death itself if the book had been accurate. And now Track remembered something else—a little item he had picked up in the *Chicago Tribune* once at O'Hare while waiting for a plane. An obituary for a writer name C. W. Morris. In the obituary they had listed the man's works, among them a book called *The Killing Machine*.

The Killing Machine was here, in Mexico, to kill him.

Track listened and waited.

The voices were just whispers, half-intelligible.

Track stood to his full height as the clouds bared the moon and he pushed the M-16 ahead of him at waist level, both fists locked on it as he fired.

A tallish, burly-looking man in dark clothes swung his Uzi toward him as Track's assault-rifle fire cut him down. Track's M-16 cut across the chest and neck and laced across the face of a second man as his shotgun discharged, rock chips spraying upward toward Track's face and hand forcing him to sidestep.

The third man fired as Track threw himself down, the fourth man backing away.

The rocks beside Track's head exploded. Track rolled onto his back, then onto his chest.

Up on his knees, Track fired, his assault rifle emptying as the clouds once more obscured the moon.

Track fell forward, rolled, then remained perfectly motionless.

He heard the whisper—and knew he was intended to hear it. There were shouts from the village below but Track couldn't make out the words. But the whisper was very clear. "Major Track, you are very good, sir. A little reckless, but very good."

"Mr. Melon," Track called back, changing to his second 30-round stick. He had sixty rounds left. "I don't know who sent you—but I can guess it was Murphy."

"Very good and very astute. Yes, Major Track, it was Mr. Murphy. He explained why you and the young lady have to die."

"Why does the young lady have to die?" Track asked, noting a slight change in the direction of Melon's voice. The old Killing Machine was in motion. Track started to move, as well, edging along the rocks.

"She is a liability, Major. After I took this assignment, I checked you out. You seem like a fine man. I read up on your military career, that deal with that crackpot Nazi. You are a very fine man, sir, but the girl must be killed and you cannot be trusted to keep quiet about it. That's the breaks."

"Why the girl?" Track repeated, crawling down into a depression in the rocks, moving laterally away from the voice and toward the village below.

"She is—how to put it—whacko? She murdered another girl—hacked her to pieces, from what I understand. It won't be long before the cops start looking for her. With her dead, the cops will be persuaded not to look and this will all be kept quiet."

"She's mentally ill, Melon. You understand that? How'd you like it when your kid died?"

"I didn't like it. But my son was a patriot. He was a fighter. He died serving his country, just like you would or I would, Major. This girl is a crazy killer."

Track closed his eyes. The pot was calling the kettle black.

"So, as a good American, what should I do, Mr. Melon?"

"If you throw down your gun, I'll kill you with one shot that you'll never feel. I promise you, Major."

"So, to be a good American, I should let you kill me."

"The needs of our country will be best served that way. Don't get me wrong. I don't expect you just to let me kill you. But I will kill you. And when I do, I'll make it quick as a flash. Honest."

"How you gonna kill the girl? Gonna nuke the village down there?"

"Then she is in the village."

"Along with Colonel Rodriguez and some of his army guys and some terrorists, I'm betting. I don't know who the hell's holed up at the end of the village street. Whoever it is must have the girl."

"Maybe the KGB. Could be them." Melon seemed excited.

Track licked his lips. "How about a truce? I want the girl out of there. And you want her dead. Neither one of us gets our way with that gunfire goin' on down there. If it lasts long enough the Mexican federal police might show up and ruin everybody's day."

"A truce? When you know full well I intend to kill you? Interesting, Major."

"Talk's cheap," Track answered, sliding down a trench in the rocks, then edging right. "Well, what about it?"

"Major Track, that's the most audacious thing anyone has ever said to me. You have a deal. A truce until the girl is away from her captors and we take care of the enemy. I understand you might not be too well armed. That M-16 all you have?"

Track laughed. "More or less."

"There are some Uzis and an 870 and some miscellaneous handguns whose owners don't need them anymore. Come ahead and shop."

Track slipped down the rest of the way in the trench and dropped to the level Melon and his three men had been on.

He heard Melon's voice behind him. "Lucky for you, Major, that we have a deal."

Track laughed. "Take a look at where the muzzle of my M-16 is pointing, Mr. Melon." Track had the M-16 pointed into the shadows, where the voice had originated.

"Touché. Come on." Track saw Melon's face as the moon cleared from the clouds. A pleasant forthright face—until you got to the eyes. Even in the semidarkness there was something there Track didn't like to see.

30

With Ralph Melon behind him—there was some comfort in knowing where the Killing Machine was but not much—Dan Track ran from shadow to shadow along the backsides of the buildings toward the target building at the far end of the street. As they had come down from the rocks, Melon told him that a computer check had produced an article in a travel magazine from 1969 that had carried a short photo story on Los Quatros Santos, touting it as a village unchanged in a century. If the village had remained unchanged since 1969, the building at the end of the street was still a cantina.

Track hoped it was; before the truce ended he wanted a drink.

Despite his sixty or so years, Melon moved better than most men in their thirties could move. He was fast, surefooted and agile.

Another of the advantages in being ahead of Melon was not having to catch up to him.

They stopped, in deep shadow, Melon rasping behind him, "Do the sprint. I'll cover you."

"How's the truce?" Track whispered.

"Fuckin' wonderful. Do the sprint, Track."

Track wasn't dressed to sprint. The M-16 was slung behind his back; he had a six-inch Colt Python in his trouser band and he held a Uzi in his fists. He did the sprint anyway, keeping to the shadows where possible, until he could flatten himself against the wall of the cantina.

The gunfire had stopped a few moments earlier.

Track covered as Melon made the sprint. It would have been easy to shoot Melon—or it seemed so—but the truce was still on.

Track heard Rodriguez's voice as Melon hit the wall beside him. "Señor Halston, it must be you."

"What the hell you want, Rodriguez?"

"I want the girl, *señor*, that your man took from the street."

"What you want with a streetwalker?" The voice laughed.

"Halston?" Track asked Melon, then answered his own question. "Los Angeles—Cosa Nostra—"

"You got it, Track," Melon murmured.

"You still feel like you're on the right side, trying to kill the girl?"

"Ask me later." Melon grinned in the moonlight, then the moon was gone, Melon's face with it, like the Cheshire cat's. Melon's voice came out of the darkness. "They probably got a guy or two lookin' out back here."

"Agreed."

"So, get up on the roof. I'll give you a boost. Once you're on the roof, we both count to twenty. I come in the back way; you use that squirt gun to cut a hole in the roof. The roof material should slow down most of the slugs, so there's not much chance of killing the girl if she's down there—in case you're interested. When they hear you on the roof, I come in the back shooting."

"Not the girl," Track warned.

"We still got a truce, Track. Remember."

Track looked at the wall, about ten feet up there were wooden poles protruding from the stucco and adobe. He imagined they acted as roof supports. They were about the diameter of a chinning bar.

Melon dropped into a crouch, cupping his hands.

Track shrugged, took a step back and shot his right leg into Melon's cupped hands as Melon lurched upward. Track's hands reached out, the Uzi free-swinging now. Track's hands connected with two of the poles. His left leg began to throb. His head was past hurting.

He started to pull himself up; when his chest was level with his fists he threw his right leg up onto the roof. If whoever was in the building had a man on the roof, Track knew there wouldn't be time to do anything except die.

His right leg up, Track braced his foot and pushed up and over onto the roof. It sagged beneath him as he started to count to twenty. At "four" he started across the roof on his hands and knees, hearing shouts from beneath him. They'd start shooting in about ten seconds, he guessed.

By "eleven" he was at the center of the roof, swinging the Uzi forward, aiming it at a spot where the roof seemed to be sagging more than elsewhere.

"Seventeen...eighteen...nineteen...twenty." Track opened up, cutting the Uzi in a circle the size of a manhole cover, emptying the magazine into the roof. As well as the screaming and shouts from beneath him, there was now gunfire from the front of the building and from near the church across the street.

He could also hear gunfire from behind him—Melon. Track ran two steps forward, jumped up and, with both feet together, crashed downward, his hands and arms protecting his face and head as the roof structure seemed to disintegrate beneath his feet.

Track opened his eyes in time to see the top of the wooden saloon table smashing under him as he threw himself forward, his hands going out for a neck and his body weight launching after his hands. He was on the floor, on top of another man. Track's head and left thigh ached in tandem as his right fist crossed a jawline and the head of the man beneath him snapped back.

Track rolled, gunfire hammering into the floor.

To the rear of the cantina, the interior yellow-lit by lamps and hanging heavy with cigar smoke, a door fell inward. Melon stepped through, a Uzi in one hand, an 870 in the other, the shotgun tearing into somebody's chest. Track pushed himself up, swung his right hand to his belt and grasped at the six-inch stainless-steel Colt .357. He had it trained on a slightly built man with unkempt dark hair who wheeled toward him, brandishing a Mauser pistol.

The face—Track's trigger finger stopped in midsqueeze.

"Major?"

"Rudy?"

"Shit—what are you—"

"Help me," Track snapped, wheeling away from Rudy, counting on the man he had met and worked with in Acapulco, the man most trusted by the old don who was now dead, not to shoot him in the back.

There were men coming through the front door now. The men wore fatigues and military uniforms devoid of insignia. Track shot the first man through the door, then the second and the third. He heard the peculiar high-pitched crack of a pistol behind him. His gamble had paid off. It was the Bolo Mauser Rudy carried.

"Major!"

Track wheeled as the fourth man through the door went down. Rudy tossed a SPAS 12 across the airspace between them. Track's left reached out and caught the ten pounds of shotgun. He found the quick-deployment safety in the trigger guard, then edged his finger back, banking on a loaded chamber.

He fired, the SPAS rocking in his hands, the noise of it earsplitting in the closed space. Three of the terrorists fell back, each with a chunk of the buckshot load in his face and chest.

The empty shucked, Track set the SPAS on semiauto mode and worked the trigger again, not knowing whether buckshot or slug would be up next. It was buckshot he fired toward the door.

Rudy was beside him now, the Broomhandle firing in little hiccups. Track wheeled away from the doorway, the hairs on the back of his neck standing to attention. He heeded his built-in warning system, throwing himself left as he turned. A man in a white leisure suit with a 66 2 1/2 in his right fist was firing toward where Track's back had been. Track fired the SPAS, the shot column catching the white-suited man at the belt line, his body jackknifing and then flying backward like a kid doing a reverse cannonball dive into a swimming pool.

He could see Melon was busy. The 870 and the Uzi were evening up the odds. Track couldn't see the girl yet.

Then he heard a scream—and a laugh.

The girl was in the far corner of the cantina. One of the fatigue-clad men from the front door was ripping her dress away with his left hand as he thrust a pistol forward toward her chest. Track heard a French-accented voice across the room. "Rodriguez—do not do this thing!"

The girl laughed—loudly.

The pistol, muzzle-flush to her left breast, discharged.

From the corner of his eye Track saw Rudy wheel toward the shot. But by then Track had the SPAS thrust forward, firing, the whole shot column hitting the man someone had called Rodriguez in the small of the back. The man's body slapped into the body of the already dead Debbie Hinchcliffe as his pistol discharged again, cutting a bloody tunnel through her throat.

The French voice again, "Don't shoot. No, Monsieur Melon—"

"Die, François. I'll write your mother a note about it!" From the far corner Melon opened up with the Uzi. Track's eyes followed the line of fire to a mud-splattered, once-well-dressed handsome young man with a fancy-looking Browning Hi-Power in his right fist. The body twitched, danced, pirouetted—then fell like a bag of cement to the floor by the door of the cantina.

Rudy ran up beside Track, shouting to him. "Outa here, Major. Move it!"

Track started for the back door. Melon did his trick with the 870 again, then threw the shotgun away.

More men were streaming through the doorway now, some of them in fatigues, others in civies—sports clothes with shoulder holsters and cartridge belts.

Rudy was through the door, ramming a fresh stripper clip into his Bolo Mauser as they hit the street, Track behind him, Melon next.

"Who the hell are you?" Melon snapped, ramming a fresh magazine up the well of his Uzi.

"Never mind," Rudy panted. "Major, what's goin' on?"

"Those your guys in the civilian clothes?"

"Yeah. But you killed Chet Halston. They won't listen to me now cause I helped you. Come on. We got cars parked by the dunes on the edge of town." Rudy started to run.

Track noticed a SPAS 12 beside a dead man and dropped to his knees. In the pockets of the man's bloodstained sport coat were shot shells—not his brand but he scooped them up anyway, stuffing them into his pockets as he ran after Rudy.

He glanced once behind him. Melon was coming.

Flames licked the cantina now, through the hole in the roof. A stray slug must have hit one of the lamps, Track thought.

He kept running, his left leg screaming in protest.

The town stopped and the desert began. Rudy was still ahead of him, the Bolo Mauser ready. Track fed shells into the tube of the SPAS as he ran.

The ground rose sharply; Track stumbled once, then picked himself up. He reached the top of the dune and followed Rudy down the other side, half running, half falling. His head hurting him very badly now, but he kept running.

Rudy was at the base of the dune now. Track threw himself down the slope, rolling, skidding to his knees, sand in his face, on his hands.

He started forward and heard a click from behind him.

Track started to bring up the SPAS as he turned.

The Uzi was aimed at his head. He could see the muzzle like a dark tunnel despite the distance. Track kept moving the SPAS on line for Melon, knowing he wouldn't make it.

"Truce is off, Track!"

The Uzi didn't fire for an instant. There was a pistol shot, then another, and Track threw himself down to the sand, the Uzi firing, not at him but over him.

Track pushed the SPAS out one-handed and fired, his wrist taking the recoil. Another item in his catalogue of pain.

Melon's body rocked, tumbled laterally across the ridge of the dune, then skidded downward, cutting a furrow in the sand that the emerging moon showed dark and wet.

Track let the shotgun fall to his side on its sling. If his life had depended on it, he couldn't have fired the shotgun again with his right hand. With his left hand he drew the stainless Python, awkwardly working the cylinder-release catch, dumping the empties then holding the open cylindered six-gun under his right arm as he searched his pockets for the loose .357s. He found what felt like six, holding the revolver against his body with his forearm, loading the cylinder.

As he closed the cylinder, he found Rudy.

Track looked back toward the top of the dune. No one was coming yet. He dropped to his knees beside Rudy. "Hey, what are you doin' savin' my life?"

Rudy opened his eyes; as he laughed, blood flecked his chin. "It seemed like a good idea at the time, Major. How's that beautiful babe Desiree, huh?"

"Just as beautiful. I'll get her to give you a big wet kiss."

Rudy laughed again. "Naw, I'll be dead, Major. Tell me—" he coughed "—were we on the right side?"

Track didn't know what to answer, but he said, "Yeah. I was down here for the U.S. government. Even though the girl died, the bad guys didn't get the information she had—so—so we won really."

"Hey, Major." Rudy's eyes closed. Track thought for an instant his friend was dead. He held the man's head against his thigh, supporting him. The eyes opened again. "I got a wife—kids. Tell my wife...give her the number tattooed on the bottom of my left foot. Tell her take away two from each of em. She'll know."

"Swiss?"

"Yeah. Enough to send the kids to college...so they don't grow up like me, huh," he said, laughing. "And tell her, well, I love her a lot...and..." He raised the Bolo Mauser.

"For your son," Track whispered, remembering the story of the gun Rudy had told him once.

Rudy nodded his head. "Son." Rudy coughed once more and his face turned away, but his eyes didn't close.

Track closed them.

Track sagged back on his haunches in the sand. He started to search Rudy's pockets. Car keys for a Ford product. Ten stripper clips, five of them still loaded. A Bolo Mauser wasn't any good, after all, without stripper clips.

The last thing Dan Track did was to read the number off the sole of Rudy's foot and memorize it. Then he started off at a loping, lopsided jog-trot toward where he hoped the cars were parked.

31

Dan Track sat in the Mercedes, his right wrist bandaged, his right arm in a sling. In his left trouser pocket was a .25 Beretta Jetfire. Since he was dressed for the summery weather of Miami, it wasn't really very practical to carry a big gun.

And there was no need for a gun at all, really.

Desiree Goth stared ahead, across the wheel of the Mercedes. She was as beautiful as always, wearing only a sundress, her bare arms stretched across the wheel. "How is your head?"

"I'm fine. I'll show you tonight."

He had just gotten out of a hospital two thousand miles away. They had traveled to Miami in her private plane.

They hadn't talked much. "Should you really go in there?" she asked him.

He hadn't completely ruled out the possibility Rudy's wife might have called her husband's former employers with whom Track wasn't too popular at the moment. He wasn't too popular with the federal government, either, and had stayed at the hospital under an assumed name.

He had driven Rudy's Ford in ever-widening circles until he found the Beechcraft Ralph Melon had arrived in. He had freed the big gray horse.

Then he had flown the plane to central Mexico, ditched it and called Desiree in Switzerland. He had started the conversation by saying, "Mommie—you'll never guess what kind of trouble I'm in now."

She had come for him, with Zulu. They smuggled him across the border and into a hospital and she left Zulu with him while she covered loose ends. Three days of Zulu hovering at his bedside had convinced him he was well enough to travel. Desiree had returned for him, with the Bolo Mauser, twice as many stripper clips as Rudy had had and even a shoulder holster for it, all wrapped in brown paper. They rewrapped the package aboard the plane.

He leaned across the center of the seat to kiss her. "It'll be fine. Just keep the motor running."

"I love you," she whispered.

"Let's do something about that," he replied, "when I get back." He worked the door handle and stepped out. Standing up fast still gave him a headache.

And the sun didn't help. He walked toward the door of the house, past the lawn that seemed just beyond the point where it needed to be trimmed.

Debbie Hinchcliffe was as dead as her alter ego, Rodriguez was dead; and Fuentes's government was in a state of collapse according to the news broadcasts he had watched on the television set in his hospital room. Melon was dead. Halston, the mob guy, was dead. And the French guy—Bastogne, probably the guy from Marseilles—was dead, too.

There was the little matter of Fernando Murphy who had set him up. But Track had no immediate plans in that direction. Murphy would have a hard enough time after U.S. Representative Miles Jefferson opened his mail and read the anonymous letter detailing the entire thing.

Senator Hinchcliffe had resigned—not only the appointment to the Intelligence Committee, but his senate seat, as well. That had been on the news, too.

Track knocked on the door, awkwardly trapping the package between the sling and his chest.

A pretty woman, her eyes too dark underneath, opened the door. She'd been crying he thought.

"Are you Rudy's wife?"

"Yes. You're Mr. Track?"

"Yes. Rudy, ah..."

"Would you like to come in?"

"All right." He walked inside and she closed the door. Inside the doorway, he stood, listening for the sounds of Rudy's children. He didn't hear them. "Kids away?"

"They're with Rudy's brother; he's an accountant."

"For the ah..."

"For a computer wholesaler."

Track nodded. He reached into his left-hand pocket and fumbled the piece of paper from beneath the Beretta there.

He handed her the piece of paper. "Swiss-bank-account number...I guess Rudy wasn't certain you had it. He said take two away from each number. It was tattooed on the bottom of his left foot."

"I had it, but Rudy was always very careful where our welfare was concerned." The woman was starting to cry.

"Ah, Rudy wanted this, for your son. A friend of mine knew Rudy, too, and got some extra things to go with it." He set the package down on the hall table.

Rudy's wife opened it slowly. "He said he wanted the money to pay for the kids going to college and that he wanted his son to...ah..."

She looked at the Bolo Mauser. Tears started to stream from her eyes. She hesitated for a moment, then leaned her head against Track's chest and wept, her body trembling.

Track folded his left arm around her and held her.

Dan Track closed his eyes.